Please note this book is a continuation of *Fighting Fire Part 1: Collusion*. For your convenience, chapters are numbered starting with Chapter 26, where *Fighting Fire Part 1: Collusion* left off.

Copyright © 2020 MÜP
All rights reserved.
ISBN: 978-1-7358254-5-8

Chapter 26

Galice didn't actually look like she'd experienced that big of a shock. Visen supposed people grieved in their own ways, of course.

She was offered fruit and warm face wipes, apparently Nadia's only two vessels for channeling mothering instinct.

They sat with her till dinner time, listening to an argument Ivle didn't realize could travel so far acoustically.

"This is kind of cool," Nadia mouthed at Visen when Galice wasn't looking.

They really could hear everything.

"No! Everyone knows that's a forgery!"

"So? So, then who does Swiverlia want so bad—"

"I think we should let Mertrian press know!"

"You're not even Mertrian!"

Was anyone here, besides Badmonkof, actually from Mertria? Or was everyone Swiverlian imports pretending to be Mertrian government?

News the president had just died would look better coming from a native Mertrian.

Smutt was from Mertria.

"No that—wouldn't make a good public image,"

Ivle knew to shut that one down. No matter how little Colby had in fact successfully conveyed regarding Ivle's machinations, the knowledge that Smutt was even remotely involved forever sealed his fate as a man who would be perpetually blocked, whenever Ivle found him trying to snivel up the political chain of command.

"Personally, I'm worried about the French…"

Nadia made a face to convey pretending she agreed wholeheartedly with this unexpected twist in the disembodied voices' train of thought. God why did Nadia have to make Visen laugh while they were trying to comfort a new widow? So *Bad*....

"Le Blanc will be watching this,"

"Le Blanc has no jurisdiction,"

"He could bring in the UN,"

"Oh please, the UN, the UN; the UN doesn't care about one fucking little Mertrian president,"

"Hey! Can you keep it down out there? We can hear you badmouthing in here!" Nadia instantly reared into mama bear. Everyone knew she was sitting with Galice.

Visen surreptitiously put an eye to her thermal imaging helmet to find the politicians had moved inconspicuously about five bedrooms further down the hall. They figured that was enough to thwart eavesdroppers.

"Don't worry," Nadia began trying to comfort Galice by awkwardly patting her back for far too long, "everyone really misses your husband,"

"I hated my husband."

"Oh."

Probably had to do with all the philandering. Nadia went back to discretely playing her match-the-cubes game, not knowing what else to do.

"Has anyone told you what we think happened to him?" Visen tried.

"Yeah. Mechanism wasn't really intended for him; it was for her,"

"Right."

"Seems a tad convenient."

"We'll keep an open mind about all other potential explanations, of course,"

"Smutt did it."

"Ah."

"Stupid little fucker."

~*~

The funeral, at least, was a bit cheerier. Mainly because more significant others were invited to attend, which meant Nadia was in her element chatting up ladies who were trying to look pretty.

Visen's tour of duty had been extended five extra days, to allay any impressions Ivle wasn't doing everything he could to protect his wife, in case rumors of her potential kidnapping had rustled their way unofficially through the insinuations surrounding Badmonkof's death.

Visen stayed close by Nadia's side, happy being a bodyguard gave her an excuse not to talk too much. Nadia took care of any awkward lulls in conversation anyway.

"So are you going to Fiji again this year?"

As it was a funeral, each topic had to be brought up in a respectfully subdued manner— which Nadia hadn't quite mastered yet. She'd chosen dead pan, with mouth slightly ajar, as her standard form of address, to give herself a blank resting face she hoped looked mournful, but which was, in fact, the closest she could ever come to looking as though she absolutely did not care about anything.

"Ah, no, California,"

"Oh yeah? That's real nice… Are you bored out of your skull?" she whispered in Visen's ear about halfway through mingling.

"It's interesting to see so many higher ups all together,"

"Yeah but they're all being purposefully boring; I know she goes to Fiji; now we know she must be going there for something covert, otherwise why try to hide it?"

"Hm."

Visen sat with the Ivles for the reception, which took the form of a dinner party. It was weird, sitting professionally with Ivle, now she knew so very many unwanted details about his sex life, especially since Ivle seemed to be the one person with whom Nadia didn't want to start up a conversation.

Ivle himself was just realizing what a horrible mistake it was to let a subordinate peak into the disaster that was his home life. But he couldn't very well let Nadia out in public without at least trying to keep up an appearance of caring for her well-being. At least Visen conveniently encapsulated in one body both the guard who witnessed their marital troubles, and the guard who'd undoubtedly been forced to listen to all his wife's conspiracy theories—in case Ivle wanted to get rid of all evidence for both simultaneously. Only one body to discard could prove useful.

The real reason for Nadia's silence was that she didn't feel comfortable sitting this close to her husband; she didn't like it when people could see her eat, that's why the overlong dining arrangements back home suited her just fine.

Now, as soon as food arrived, she began peckering self-consciously after some form of conversation to keep Ivle from noticing how loudly she swallowed— she just couldn't help it; she couldn't do it quietly. She'd even looked up a surgery once to get it fixed.

"Evelle, have you ever been to Fiji?"

"What?"

"Fiji. Eppie Volcraft was saying—"

"Oh my God—no Nadia," Ivle continued skimming dinner guests anxiously. "Krakoveen isn't here." He didn't think his reputation could take the hit if it was found Smutt's suspicions— of all peoples'—concerning Krakoveen's guilt were well-founded. That might make make his suspicions of Ivle look well-founded as well.

Unfortunately, all the dignitaries who could have reassured Ivle on this point were actively avoiding him, on account of his wife. They'd heard the arguing over inopportune phone calls to her sister Marge—to say nothing of being told off for gossiping close enough Galice could hear. Nadia'd become something of a pariah for the moment.

But it was worse— (Visen began calculating): everyone was acting as though they all feared they were next to be assassinated. How much of this was simply attempting to avoid saying anything controversial, in a bid to seem worthy of replacing Badmonkof?

All the monosyllabic quietude was beginning to freak Nadia out.

She scanned the tables round them, anxiously idle, until she finally seized on the nearest living diners outside her own party, a young couple half a table's length away. "Are you two recently engaged?" she leaned over, all friendly aunt-like. "I couldn't help but notice—the ring; it's so pretty!" The couple'd been sitting very tensely, pointedly holding hands across the table as though unaccustomed to politics.

"Oh," both snapped out of their reverie, "yes, yes we are,"

"Yeah? That's so nice,"

Ivle repositioned, irritated Nadia had still managed to find some form of inanity to drivel.

"Are you from Mertria? Politicians?"

"Ah, no, I'm related to Badmonkof actually, just a civil servant—I'm his niece,"

"Oh I'm so sorry,"

"Oh, that's okay; I didn't know him very well."

Nadia continued watching her expectantly.

They hadn't brought out plates for the next dinner course yet. There wasn't much else to do.

Badmonkof's niece began to feel as though she were obliged to keep talking. "I'm… honestly more worried about what it means next for Mertria, we're—well, you know, we don't have the most stable track record," the niece smiled regretfully at her other half.

"Ye-eah, well, don't worry; it'll work out. My husband's actually trying to help broker peace right now; this is my husband, Evelle. It's so nice meeting young love. Remember when we were like that? Evelle?"

"Yeah."

Nadia was only a few years older than the bride to be.

"Sorry, I need to go see uh—" Ivle excused himself to go bend over an elder statesman at the head table running the width of the hall, which promised more politically acute discussion by hosting important Mertrian personnel.

No-o-o please don't leave! Visen found herself internally squinching into horrified abandonment. Surprise! Scary bosses were better than making small talk about wedding rings. Now Visen was all alone.

"Was it a recent engagement?"

Visen kept staring straight ahead.

"Ah, yeah, yup; just two weeks ago now; we're— very much in love,"

"Aww! That's so sweet! And it only gets better, you know; you get more and more connected," Nadia somehow managed to look as though she actually meant it. "I tell you what; y'know, we're technically hosting— I'm gonna order some champagne for you, to celebrate, have a little bit of something good on the house, after—"

"Nadia, what?"

"—no, no really you don't need to go out of your way—"

"No, no especially after a loved one's died; you need to be pampered; you guys are newlyweds— almost! That's so exciting; you want some lobster? You guys deserve a fancy dinner. You like lobster?" (the main dinner dish was supposed to be salmon. But chefs always kept tabs on the location of any fresh lobster for Nadia within a thirty-mile vicinity in case she ever got peckish; it was just one of those things multi-millionaires can demand.)

"Nadia—" Ivle clapped someone on the back in a bid to move closer and circumvent his wife— her voice could carry naturally over two football fields; it was impossible not to hear her over everyone else's chatter.

Why was Visen just sitting there allowing this? *Potential Leakage!* He gave Visen a look, then back to Nadia: "what are you doing?"

"What? You supplied security," that meant they had access to the kitchens. She shifted her gaze between husband and Visen, both of whom were looking a little uncomfortable at the thought of celebrating nuptials at a funeral.

"Yeah I don't think—"

"I'm gonna order you some champagne, take those worries away,"

"Oh—no—"

"Of course! It's not like it's a big deal! You need something to pick you up! come on Visen; we'll be right back; I'm just gonna check with the kitchen to make sure they can get some—"

Ivle was left looking blotchily ostrich-like.

As soon as they were far enough away not to be heard, Nadia motioned Visen closer to whisper, "there's something wrong; that engagement ring's fake. See? Look, it doesn't sparkle, the way mine does."

"Nadia—"

"Should I tell her?"

"No, I don't think—"

"I'm gonna see if I can figure out what's going on,"

"They may just not have a lot of money,"

"Go get the lobster; I'll try to drag it out of them—but keep your radio on and get your gun ready; I think it might be a ploy!" Nadia was looking thrilled.

"Ehhh…"

"What? They need to be by themselves with me to feel comfortable opening up so I can catch them off guard; come on, go go go!"

"I don't know if—oi, Wheeler?" Visen radioed to where her second in command for the evening was slouching through front-door duty. "Keep an eye on Nadia for a moment, will you?" She began plowing sideways through scuffed chairs towards the kitchens. Nadia'd already returned to their dining table.

Fortunately, Visen'd left her phone on the table—it had a built-in recorder; that was the radio by which Nadia meant to transmit to Visen's handheld. Not very technologically savvy, but they'd dreamed it up just in case they got momentarily separated. Nadia thought it was more socially elegant than gallivanting around screaming professionalism through walkie talkies. Visen turned the headset by her ear to the proper channel for listening in:

"Ah-heh, aah, yeah, college, yeah. We met in college,"

They weren't enjoying being grilled. Visen never knew Nadia could be so aggressively comforting.

"Aw, that's so sweet," Nadia played imperceptive. "What college did you go to?"

Why did Visen feel like Nadia'd dreamed this up to replace not being able to investigate why Eppie Volcraft refused to admit she'd been to Fiji?

She went to order lobster stoically.

"Amherst; do you know—?"

"Oh, yeah, I've heard of that!"

"Yeah; I'm, very glad he's here with me today,"

Visen could practically hear lovers' smiles through the headset.

"Aww, so, do you have a dress picked out yet?"

"Ah—yeah, here, it's not a picture of me in the dress but I'll pull it up—" Another pause.

"Oh, my gawd it's so beautiful; that'll look so good on you! I just knew when I saw you guys; I could tell how much you were in love,"

Visen started back towards the luncheon, lobster procured. Wheeler gave a nod from where he'd positioned himself to watch over Nadia in her absence.

"Well we, we really wouldn't want to impose on y'all; we weren't actually planning on staying more than a few minutes—"

"Oh no, come on, stay for lobster at least—it'll be out soon!" Nadia was signaling with reckless abandon in the form of vigorous eye contact that something was wrong with them.

That, Visen realized, would probably be the concealed pistol Badmonkof's niece had shoved down one boot.

Right.

"It's just we promised to meet a friend—He just texted; he's at the front bar; we were just gonna go collect him—"

"Oh, yeah, no of course, bring him over; we can all have lobster together!"

"Yeah, sounds good,"

"We'll be right back,"

"I'm actually thinking of asking him to be my best man,"

"Aw! good luck!"

Frantic signals for Visen to follow.

"Right." Visen dipped aside to peer round a tent flap just in time to see the fiancé retrieve a silenced FNX-45 tactical from a fern. *Ah-hah.*

They were heading for the exit just past— Ivle.

They got within three paces of him before Badmonkof's 'niece' drew her gun, almost unnoticeable to the crowd; her 'fiancé' blocked it from view. She held it at her hip; it wasn't for bullets; that'd be a tranquilizer, or—

"Freeze! Drop it!" from the pivot of her wrist, Visen could tell she'd aimed it at the small of Ivle's spine, exposed, as it was, below the back of his folding chair.

The niece fired anyway, but not before Visen grabbed her gun—a dart ripped through the tent's tarp, trajectory askew; Visen shoved her to the ground, just as the fiancé whipped out his

FNX and aimed at Visen's face. A smart kick up launched the gun to one side and gave Visen the momentum needed to stand from where she'd half-tackled the fiancée, to punch fiancé in the face. Then she back kicked when the fiancée tried to stand under her. Fiancé swung back. She caught at the punch and snapped his wrist, tilting the gun out of his grasp and rounding into a headlock.

"Don't move," she held her gun to his head, but the fiancée was already streamlining her gun's aim towards Ivle again. Visen knocked the fiancé out with his own gun and lurched over him to smash the fiancée's hands to one side. The poisonous little viper of an easily disintegrable sting launched itself into the grass just beyond Ivle's left leg instead of into it.

It'd all happened so fast he was still considering yelling at Visen for over-reacting.

Nadia was looking thrilled.

"Alright,"

Her coolest lover to date resurfaced with a bloodied lip and the venom-spitting tranquilizer gun securely held beyond Badmonkof's niece's reach. The niece's arms were pinned by Visen's left knee; her hip pushed to the ground by Visen's right. She wasn't going anywhere.

Oh man Nadia'd give anything to be under that deadlock.

"What happened?"

"We'll get the information from him when he wakes," Visen nodded Wheeler over to take the collapsed fiancé off their hands, then jerked round to bring the fiancée to her feet, hands behind her back; kneed again into keeping perfectly still by a perfectly placed leg against her spinal column. She didn't look like she was about to do any talking.

Visen didn't have any handcuffs.

"Jeffers!" Visen recognized one of the gradually encroaching security guards from Super Bowl Sunday. "Handcuffs?"

"Yeah, yeah," he hurried over, to ineffectually round up the concussed assassins.

It was only after handcuffs were in place that Visen realized the luncheon had kind of been ruined. People were standing, curiosity having gotten the best of their urge to run, all round the sides of the open-air tent, ready to book it should anyone else draw a gun, having already upset quite a few tables and chairs. Absolute silence reigned.

"Right," she raised her eyebrows at Nadia and grimaced cartoonized recognition of her own awkwardness.

Thank God Nadia, at least, laughed.

"I don't see what's so funny."

Oh Ivle. Ruiner of everything.

"Sorry sir I was making a face."

Well if he was gonna be so juvenile as to complain at his wife for laughing after a traumatic event, he'd get the juvenile answer he deserved.

"Should we call the local constabulary, or would you like federal agents to take care of this?" Wheeler peered round from behind Ivle's back.

"I don't—"

"Should probably make it federal agents."

Local constabulary had lost the last man they'd taken into custody. Wheeler nodded and went off to call Fetchins.

"Well," Ivle tried to regain authority, "that is, precisely what I wanted you to do, Visen. So, thank you."

"They weren't targeting your wife though, sir. They were targeting you,"

"Well yes I—" well, he had sort of noticed that. "Are you sure about that?" It could have been a ruse.

Visen lifted the nearest clean plate and ran it through the grass below his table to pick up the capsule snagged into the dirt by Badmonkof's niece's gun. She let it tinkle into the middle of the porcelain, dirt crumbling, then held it up to eye level.

"I'll see what's in this, then we'll know." something to make the victim sleep, with a delayed onset to the drug's effects—that'd mean a kidnapping attempt. Otherwise.... "Until we know for sure I think you should go back to your house." Stay inside.

Ivle's mansion wasn't too far from the funereal luncheon.

Visen had a chemical identification kit she kept with her more advanced gear in the rucksack in her room.

Chapter 27

Thirty minutes later, little strips like litmus paper came out of Visen's bag to be dipped in the fiancé's now smashed vial, each coated with traces of identifiers to see what chemical compositions could be identified by the changes in color that'd run up their sides.

Visen snapped pictures to record the reactions. "Arsenic," she tightened her lips in an apologetic, mercurial frown as Nadia entered the room.

"Oh my God. So, they are after the politicians!"

"Well."

Why did no one like Visen's original analysis that the meshy bag which killed Badmonkof had obviously been meant to trap Nadia? So, they weren't after politicians, they were after the Ivles. Although, Visen supposed she could never be sure....

"I wonder if that means they want Ivle to be the next interim president," Nadia mused.

"Like a—test?"

The phone in Visen's room rang. It was Ivle, laconic as ever: "my office. now."

"Don't tell him anything about Desmond trying to break in, right?" Nadia hissed after her as she left.

"Why?"

"He could get fired,"

Oh man.

~*~

"Sir?" Visen appeared in Ivle's office two minutes later.

"Tell me more about that break in you experienced while I was gone,"

"—Yes sir." She'd assume that meant the frogman, not Desmond. "Did you want me to tell you about the capsule they shot at you?"

"Not now."

"It contained arsenic,"

"Yes, that's not what I'm worried about, right now. What happened during the break in?"

How was he not— worried?

Visen explained as best she could the movements of the 17 intruders from that past Friday, their combat with Wheeler, and how she had noticed the antiquated frogman gear, along with their peculiar sweep and search tactics, which seemed to indicate they were searching for someone, and hadn't been trained by any official military to do so.

"Did they take anything?"

"No."

"But you think they left the net,"

"They could have. They were everywhere."

"Where did you keep my wife?"

Uh-oh.

"Visen?"

Well, it had been Desmond, not the secret hideaway, that first came to Nadia's mind when thinking of things not to tell her husband.

Visen could only assume that meant Nadia never used the hide-away in her bathroom to hide from Ivle himself.

And if she did, Visen'd help her build a new, un-compromised safe room. Or, get her the fuck out of here; the idea crossed her mind for the first time now. Nadia was smart; Nadia had saved the day twice now. She was wasted, on matching cube games, of all things.

"She has a safe room behind the panels in her bathroom wall."

"What?"

"She installed it herself. It saved both our lives."

"Show me."

"Alright."

Visen led the way round to Nadia's bathroom, feeling trapped.

She could only hope Nadia wasn't using the little cubby hole to spy as they spoke.

But Nadia wasn't in her own room; she was still upstairs, in Visen's, reading how to use the military grade chemical strips. She watched through the surveillance panel in Visen's floor instead, as Visen led Ivle across to her bathroom's secret cubby hole and pried it's sliding panel up with one swoop to show Ivle the darkened interior. It was simply bad luck Nadia'd recently used the little place and forgotten to replace the segment of paneling that covered her keyhole.

So. Ivle blinked. That was how Nadia'd heard all about rigged elections, nuclear reactor blueprints—hidden paperwork—and that was only the most recent salvo she'd reported to Jacobsan (and which Jacobsan, of course, as always, had reported back to Ivle).

This was definitely going in the divorce papers.

"Alright. Thank you Visen."

They went back round to his not-so-secret, now officially known to be compromised office. "So that was your idea, the— hiding spot?"

"Uh, no, Nadia installed that herself, a while back, in case of break-ins."

Even as Visen said it, it struck her as an oddly paranoid precaution, for someone who usually spent all day matching cubes together. She could see the ticking over that came of reevaluating a wife Ivle'd always thought he knew, creasing momentarily through his consciousness.

"Alright." He decided. "I'm going to need to keep you with us for a few more days."

"You wouldn't like me to follow up on the assassination attempt?" She'd already traced the origin of the arsenic to Beirut. She could—

"No. That's all been taken care of." That sort of follow up was what one used Swiverlian Secret Services for, not lone SEALS.

"I just want you to continue keeping an eye on Nadia, for the next few days. It's crucial she does not use that cubby hole to spy on me. Understand?" There were things he didn't want even Jacobsan knowing about. "I'm sure you noticed it seems a bit too aptly able to spy on my home office."

"Oh, I think that's just a coincidence sir; it helped a lot to have a means of looking out, otherwise I'd never have seen our attackers' uniforms; I was too busy keeping Nadia out of the way."

"Yeah, well, I'm sure the peephole was set up to catch me cheating, for her solicitor," —*if she ever figures out she needs one;* Ivle snapped the lapels of his jacket forward to straighten himself, obviously uncomfortable.

"Ah." Visen nodded.

"But I don't need to remind you, my wife's levels of situational awareness aren't the brightest. Jacobsan—that's our—family lawyer—says she's come up with quite a few interesting accusations, which I'm sure she's told you all about. Can you tell me, what all she has told you, exactly, about what she thinks I've been up to?"

Visen could sense a trap. The house was undoubtedly bugged. He must be trying to gauge her trustworthiness.

"She told me you planned to plant some blueprints on Livonia, or Mertria, I can't remember. I figured at the time it was a bit of a conspiracy theory, you know, to keep herself entertained. Although, I suppose it could correspond to my last courier job, somehow, if she's gotten things a bit garbled. She seems to have overheard something while you were speaking to your lawyer; I had the impression it was while you were all at dinner." There, now Nadia couldn't be blamed for spying.

"Alright." Ivle nodded, thinking clouded, but trust in Visen intact. "I want you to report to me everything she tells you, about me and my operations, over the next few days. I want to know precisely what it is she thinks she knows. And Visen? Keep her from babbling, even to security, will you?" he'd seen footage of their impromptu Superbowl party.

"Yes Sir."

"You'll sleep in her room while I'm still here. Make sure she doesn't sneak away during the night to spy on me, alright? I'll set you up with a cot by the bathroom. I want you on her, Visen, 24/7,"

Oh God. Such an inadvertently on-point pun.

"Yes sir."

At least Visen could tell by the cavalier way he said it — despite all the security cameras— Ivle didn't seem to know she and Nadia were sleeping together.

Not, of course, that Nadia'd desire intimacy with Visen again any time soon, once she found out what Visen'd told Ivle.

Chapter 28

"See? I told you he doesn't sleep in the same room with me usually. It's so he can cheat on me," Nadia was still waiting in Visen's room, when she finally came back upstairs, dismissed from the confines of Ivle's only CCTV-free office.

"You heard us?"

"Through the surveillance panel."

"Oh." Visen hadn't known there was a surveillance panel in her room that opened down onto Ivle's office.

And here she'd been feeling bad Nadia couldn't go anywhere without being seen. "I'm sorry I showed him your secret room,"

"That's okay." The cabinet under the sink sported an identical panel concealing an identical secret chamber just to the right of the one Visen had compromised. That's where Nadia'd actually been watching them from, this time round (she'd figured she should listen in to the rest of the interview, once she'd seen Visen blab about her infidelity-finding hide-out).

There were a lot of false cabinets in Ivle's study.

Visen could kind of tell this was probably the case, from how casually Nadia took the news her hide-away had been compromised.

She had so many questions.

She spent the afternoon staring at page 95 in Moby Dick, without reading a thing, while Nadia bubbled away in the Solarium— a bit late with her morning routine; she'd been delayed by all the spying.

So why would Nadia install secret compartments?

And why wasn't Ivle more concerned about an attempt on his life?

Well, Visen supposed, if Ivle really was head of Swiverlian Secret Services, as Nadia claimed, he'd have one of the largest police forces in the world at his disposal. That could certainly explain nullifying an entire conspiracy so quickly he no longer had any cause for concern.

Course, the secret services hadn't exactly gotten round to doing much when it came to tracking down Badmonkof's killers, but that was probably just how bureaucracy worked. When their own bureaucrats were on the line, response and resolution would no doubt approach instantaneousness in comparison to how they responded when mere presidents of Semi-Autonomous Republics were killed.

But if Nadia'd been telling the truth about Ivle's position in the Swiverlian secret service— no exaggerations, no misunderstandings— an actual slip of classified information— did that mean Ivle was so quick to discredit the rest of her conspiracy theories precisely because he knew she might actually be on to something?

Should Visen be combing through that top-secret study for whatever incriminating paperwork Nadia swore Ivle stashed 'behind' his desk?

But Ivle wasn't some rogue, independent contractor off in a hill-side lair somewhere; he really did work for OPSAI. If he was head of Swiverlian secret services too, that would only reinforce the fact that his prerogative was to achieve lasting peace. All dubious terminations of Bravos and assorted underlings aside, why plant paperwork to exacerbate the problems his politics tried to fix? It wasn't like there weren't legitimate kerfuffles between Mertria and Livonia, if he simply needed to make himself look good by smoothing things out for other politicians.

And Nadia was the same witness who'd claimed she'd taken part in an orgy that included a stolen Bengal tiger.

There were rumors Mertrian politicians fucked bears sometimes, but where would Ivle even get a Bengal tiger?

And why had Nadia lied about where she was planning to meet Badmonkof?

Visen sat analyzing until the dinner gong rang and she was forced to the inevitable conclusion that the only eating arrangement more awkward than dining all the way across that impossibly long table from Nadia, was being forced to sit smack dab in its middle while Ivle and wife glared silent daggers at one another down its length from either side.

This was definitely about Visen's betrayal of the secret hide-away, wasn't it?

Nadia didn't appreciate the intrusion on her privacy. Ivle didn't appreciate the intrusion on his privacy the intrusion on her privacy had discovered.

"I'll be going to Swiverlia tomorrow," were practically the only words he said all evening. And Visen, hoping to err on the side of over-professional, didn't feel comfortable asking polite follow-up questions.

Nadia ate her fruit in sticky, two-inch-finger-nailed silence.

~*~

It came almost as a relief for Visen to strip down into her spandex and tank top and nudge under the reams of costly silk brocade Nadia'd piled atop the cot Ivle'd supplied, to guard her bathroom.

"Silk's good for your complexion," Nadia'd explained. Visen could've guessed.

As soon as the lights were off, she could feel the warmth of Nadia's polyester sexcapade in the form of lingerie slink over to wiggle two perkily questioning breasts against the only shoulder Visen hadn't covered in duvet. "Sooo what do you think? You wanna maybe migrate over to my bed? Make sure I don't sneak past by holding on to me tight all night?

Nadia'd managed to suppress the twang of sadness she told herself was unfounded when it came to Visen betraying her secrets to Ivle. It was Visen's job to report that sort of thing; Nadia knew that. She overcompensated by being very eager and turning off the bit of herself that was more ready to trust, replacing it with sexual appetite instead.

"Isn't Ivle in the room right next door to us?" Visen had seen him lock himself into his office for important telephone conversations after dinner.

"He made sure the walls are real soundproof on purpose." Nadia didn't slip out of her bedroom voice.

"I dunno…"

"No seriously, I've tried moaning my guts out in here while he was on the phone with Swiverlia just to fuck with him; doesn't work; he can't hear a thing." Visen bundled the duvet up round her neck defensively at the mental image anyway. "Here; watch,"

Nadia went into the bathroom and lifted up the back panel to the towel cupboard.

"Nadia! What the fuck!"

"Sh shh! He can't hear, look," Nadia made a purposefully overly-innocent little moan.

"Nadia! I've been lying my ass off for you—get—stop spying—!"

"Nadia."

They could certainly hear that through the wall, loud and clear.

Ivle'd opened the faux cabinet on the hideaway's other side to find his wife slinking.

"Just testing sir," Visen's face bobbed down into view (she'd had no idea the cabinet itself actually opened).

"Testing what?"

"To see if you can, pick up on the— wall, now—won't happen again; goodnight," she saluted an awkward para-military grimace and tried lugging Nadia back out again. The faux cabinet door snapped closed. Ivle went back to talking to the Swiverlian president.

"See he can hear everything—"

"No; it's just 'cause there're surveillance cameras in my room, so he knew I'd be in there!"

"Are there cameras in your bathroom?!" Had Ivle already known about the hideaway? CCTV live feed may've been down the day that frogman came, but that didn't necessarily mean the CCTVs themselves hadn't been recording. Did he know they'd popped out from having sex with barely nothing but a bra on between them?

"No; I set up a scented candle in front of the camera they have in here and they didn't feel comfortable admitting they wanted me to move it."

"They?"

"Y'know, Ivle and security. So, if we stay in here," Nadia mouthed, "we can have as much fun as you want; we just have to make sure we're extra quiet!" She pulled Visen down to sit beside her on the cool tile floor.

"Oh-kay…" Visen mouthed. At least it would ensure Nadia didn't learn any more about Ivle to spout off at the next opportunity. Holding her tight all night really did seem like just about the only way to distract her from spying.

That's how Visen would justify herself.

"So, what do you want to—"

Nadia stopped her with a kiss, closer and closer until she'd kneaded Visen's tank top up off her shoulders, hand slipping between Visen's skin and spandex.

"Lean round me," Nadia pressed against the wall, dress hiking till it curved round both sides of her thong. Visen fumbled it aside, hands pressed now over both Nadia's thighs, searching subtle dips round her along the perfectly shaved softness leading down Nadia's arching form to the warmth between her legs.

"Just play 'gainst me," Nadia's inhale shortened at the press of Visen's grasp from behind, the fold of her own undulating rise to arousal against the back of Nadia's thigh.

The feel of Visen's kiss against her back had buckled her senses to the slow and gentle play along her lower lips, lifting perfect swirls round nerves too used to faking pleasure.

"Oh—" Nadia's hands kneaded against the wall; she could feel the wetness of Visen's own arousal against her leg, the shake of beating hearts and rubbing warmth flowed in to one unstoppable twine.

Now they were on the floor, Visen's arms wrapped round Nadia, flush against the perfection of her spine's indent along her back, legs straddled round her thigh, the better to kiss down and along her stomach, knees not even complaining against the hardness of the floor, not now.

Visen's turn came hot and sudden, arching back, biting to keep in a moan, then panting in the subtle build to ecstasy, shaken in waves of pleasure for a miniature eternity until collapsing to curl against cool tiles, legs entwined.

About twenty minutes later—or an hour, Visen didn't know, she opened her eyes with all the brilliance of waking from a catnap, to find Nadia'd curled half under her, to lay her head across her chest. "You wanna go back to bed?"

"Hm? What should we say we were doing in the bathroom? Just talking?"

"Bedroom light's on a switch; it'll've turned off by now; CCTVs won't pick up anything in the dark; it'll look like we just went back to bed; I can turn it off for sure when we go out," the bathroom light had never been turned on.

They curled against each other; playing as they rose to sit against the bathroom wall, neither actually wanting to stand and leave.

"I never got a chance to thank you for not being mad, y'know, when—" Nadia went from sexy to suddenly avoiding eye contact, playing a finger over Visen's ribs as more of a distraction now. "Like we've only known each other what? 12 days or so? but I feel like I actually—you know, know you—" as they leaned beside the sink's dark form, Nadia's whisper felt like it encapsulated the whole world, "you know, how like— you can go years and years and only meet someone's personality, but you need something big and crazy and stupid to happen to take them outside of it, actually see who they are, you know? I like the person you are."

"I like you too," Visen really needed a new response to Nadia's professions—just a single phrase besides this derpy 'I like you too.' Surely, Visen could think up something better than that. But she was remembering now the man on the other side of the bathroom's wood paneling, who'd been right to try to protect his wife's life. "You know, it is just my job to—you know, be there more for you; Ivle's—maybe even better than me; he could show you he really loved you too, he just, you know, doesn't have the chance to hide out with you when Frenchmen attack or politicians steal documents all the time—he's busy,"

"No, I was talking about how you didn't treat me any differently after you'd found out I'd slept with a lot of people."

"Oh." That was the biggest, craziest situation?

"Like I remember, my third husband divorced me 'cause I cheated on him with this prize fighter he was grooming. So anyway, then I went to stay with the prize fighter. But he turned out to be really paranoid, like he beat me up in the bathroom of a pub, but it was in this town where I didn't really know anyone, 'cause I'd just moved out there to be with my husband, so I didn't have anyone to call except my ex-husband, but he wouldn't pick up even though I kept leaving voicemails and sending him messages, like he knew what was going on I was like 'hey, my boyfriend just punched me repeatedly into a bathroom stall and I don't have any money on me and I don't have anywhere to stay for the night and I don't know the number for a taxi' –and this was before smart phones; and he definitely saw the texts 'cause he posted them on this little friend group network chat we used to have going around and people were like 'congratulations dude! You really dodged a bullet; showed her; way to be a man!' and no all it showed me is that he was a vindictive little child who didn't have the capacity to be a husband in the first place, because I was scared; my life was in danger, that was a bad part of town, I had nothing to protect me from having to roam the streets, and be raped and murdered, and I was with someone who wanted to do both to me. But his pride was hurt so he didn't care my life could be at stake because he couldn't see that maybe breaking someone's heart isn't in the same league with letting them be raped and die in a strange city all alone at night. Like, if you can't step outside yourself for even one evening to do right by someone even though they don't deserve it, then don't you dare say you're some big macho, overcoming maturity. Sorry—that was a bit of a buzzkill wasn't it? It's just I don't get to talk to people a lot about it, y'know?"

"Nadia—"

"But like—so what I'm trying to say is fuck that shit about what they tell you you need to be to be a man—you're the best— person I've ever been with,"

Well, it wasn't exactly the most knowledgeably liberated acceptance of lesbian sexuality as a concept, but at least Visen now knew why Nadia wasn't phased by home intruders; she'd already seen the worst people had to offer.

"I'm so—"

"Sorry-y— that was a bit of a buzz kill wasn't it?"

"No, it was, actually, very perceptive."

Nadia was the sort of person who'd come back round to that 'actually' when her brain was spiraling depression and hooking grasps at further proof she lived her life unloved. But she didn't catch it at the moment, because at the moment she could tell by the look in Visen's eyes, that she hadn't meant to be belittling; she'd meant 'actually' as a contradiction to Nadia's worries.

"See, when I told Ivle that he said it was all my fault and I deserved it. Because he's stupid. He's so stupid. —Yeah obviously it was my fault! That doesn't make my ex any more in the right! —And it affects his politics too. You go about saying people deserve the shit they've been through then what are you even doing in politics?"

"Nadia?"

"Mm?"

"I'm sorry I showed Ivle your hiding spot."

"No, no that's okay, really,"

"I panicked; I didn't know what else to do; I thought he was testing me."

"Yeah no I figured it was something like that," Nadia'd grown to expect she couldn't trust anyone. That's why she always kept one step ahead of her lovers. That's why she had all those secret hiding spots in her bathroom. "I tell you what. I think we're being quiet enough; if we go back out now, we can fuck each other all over wherever we want, 'cause the CCTV's too grainy to pick up any movement with my blackout curtains across the window and the lights off. And if they do have audio it won't come out if you promise to be very very quiet," she whispered with an undulating roll against Visen's side.

"I'll be quiet," Visen meant it in lieu of promising she'd never hurt Nadia, or let her be hurt, to let them pass out of the conversation the way Nadia seemed to want to.

"Yeah?"

"Yeah, I won't make any noise,"

"Alright; I was googling ways to orgasm simultaneously earlier today; you wanna try one?"

~*~

Visen really was doing fine, when it came to keeping quiet— until she climaxed again, then she couldn't help but groan.

They could hear footsteps.

Both instantly froze, until the footsteps faded back down the hall. It was Ivle, leaving for Swiverlia.

"I thought you were supposed to be good at sneaking around!"

"That wasn't me groaning!" *Was it?*

"That was definitely you groaning!"

"Ah shit,"

Visen could only feel the tug of Nadia's arms round her middle, as they folded, the lush and heat of pillows having sent her gushing into snuggled sleepiness.

What Visen didn't realize was that Ivle was the 'third ex-husband,' the one Nadia'd cheated on with the prize-fighter. Nadia just hadn't wanted to bad mouth him in front of one of his employees. It seemed self-serving, and that hadn't been why she brought the story up. They hadn't gotten divorced; he hadn't dodged the bullet. That prize fighter'd been her revenge for his refusal to discuss anything business-related whenever she so much as entered the room. If he didn't see her as a person; if he saw her only as a sex object, then sex object she would be.

They just hadn't talked about it afterwards. She'd walked to a hotel, sheltered under its awning till two AM (no money with which to purchase a room), and then walked the seven miles home— and let a wedge grow between herself and that particular friend group. That was why she had so much spare time to play Cube Bashers.

Chapter 29

About six the next morning, Visen's cell phone started vibrating clattered jiggles across the bathroom's tile floor, from where she'd placed it by her cot the night before.

"Oh my gawd whyyy?!" Nadia plunked her head in the middle of an impossibly plush pillow and flopped another over her face so she couldn't hear.

"Sorry," Visen sneaked off to retrieve it. "Hello?" She left the room to pace the hallway, grabbing her gun on second thought and leaving the door open to keep that ever constant eye on Nadia.

"Just checking in. My wife didn't cause any trouble last night?"

"No sir. We stayed in the bathroom a while after you left, to discuss why it's important she not spy on you for the time being. I gave her my word you weren't seeing anyone on the sly. I think she gets the point, sir."

"Good. Keep it that way. You didn't notice anything odd last night?"

"Um. I think your wife may have been having a wet dream; other than that, nothing."

"Alright. I've booked her tickets for a ceremony I'll be taking part in, three days from now on October 3rd. You're to accompany her. I need her on the podium with me when I make my acceptance speech. You'll stand directly behind her, at all times. You can fly the chopper over. Frauzer,"—the Swiverlian capital— "is where you'll be headed. I'm staying at the Hotel Buckensken, you can meet me there. You'll have to stop and refuel in Dresmon; my pilot knows what to do."

"Sir, should I be the one to fly the helicopter, in case we can't trust the pilot?"

See, this was what Ivle liked about Visen. She didn't even ask what ceremony he was taking part in.

"Yes, that'll be fine if you prefer. Starts at 10:30 am. Be there the night before to go over dress protocol."

"Yes sir."

She scribbled down the dates, times, and locations. Now to find out where helipads—or, barring that, airfields— were located in the Swiverlian capital. She could ask the pilot who usually flew for Ivle, of course, but she wanted independent confirmation she wasn't flying into a trap. It was, after all, someone close to the Ivles who was after Nadia's blabbermouth, if they'd managed to break in, codes and all— even if Evelle hadn't recognized his would-be assassins at Badmonkof's funeral. Pilot could theoretically have provided information about the mansion's security codes.

At least Visen was beginning to sense why an assassination attempt had occurred.

An acceptance speech, in Swiverlian bureaucracy, could mean either an award or a promotion. And Visen couldn't think of any particular awards Ivle'd slated himself recently to receive. But you didn't need tickets to attend a normal promotional ceremony; those were only open to high command.

In fact, the only post Visen could think of, that was open at this time, and which required a ceremonial acceptance speech— and which would be important enough to trigger authorizing use of whatever forces had stamped out Ivles' fears of a repeated assassination attempt so quickly— was the post recently vacated by Badmonkof.

If Nadia's conspiracy theories were correct, Interim President of Mertria seemed like precisely the sort of power a politician playing semi-autonomous states against one another would hope to eventually wield.

But Visen couldn't believe the head of OPSAI, blackmailer or not, would kill for a presidency. Whatever Ivle's methods, he had always seemed genuine in his engagement, genuinely hurt at her treasonous activities, precisely because he valued Mertria's statehood. He simply lived in a world where the rights of individuals to freedom were not a priority.

And even then, for all his blackmail, Ivle had never double crossed Visen; he'd always kept up his end of the bargain. That was one of the horrific things about blackmail; it was like a built in Stockholm syndrome.

It would have been so much easier for him to simply spill the beans, get her kicked out of the SEALS, backed into an unemployable corner. But no. He'd kept her secret, shifting internal mechanisms of power instead to use her for missions, manipulating aside the military's prior claim on her time.

Those who were unused to such underhanded tactics in politics were simply spoiled, or naïve.

No, Ivle was honorable, in his blackmail. And that made Visen feel, at least, whether he actually was after the interim presidency or not, it was still morally safe to work with him. Or was she just excusing her own fear that if she told anyone about the general malaise of suspicion she always felt around Ivle, he'd take down what little remained of her own career as retribution?

"Who was it?"

"Ivle. He says he wants us in Frauzer in three days, to attend an acceptance speech he's making."

"What's he accepting?"

"I don't know, really; I can't be sure."

"I bet they're gonna make him Mertria's interim president."

What the—? Visen began to realize how fully she remained an outsider when it came to understanding elite bureaucratic canoodling.

"Awwwhh he's gonna make everyone listen to presentations about his charity work,"

"Mmm; well, whatever it is he wants you there,"

"Ugh," Nadia flopped back down and folded her pillow burrito back over her face.

Good answer.

Alright.
Visen went to go beg the chef to put on bacon.

Chapter 30

"But I don't even know what to wear to an inauguration," Nadia was looking through her closet, "I mean, everyone's usually so old they wear like business suits but I'm not going to wear a two-piece; that makes me look like death and accents my wrinkles,"

"What about the eh— the dress you had on when you went to visit—" Badmonkof? Oh no wait. That would send a weird message to all forty or so high-power politicians who'd seen her wearing it the night he died. Odd how political clothes could be.

"I think we should go early and see what's in fashion there," Nadia ducked into the bathroom and began running water.

Visen had taken up residence on the cot in the bedroom, plugging away at reading about whale blubber again. Second time through, she was beginning to make sense of—

"Nadia?" she surfaced suddenly. The bathwater'd been running for too long— "Are you in the—?"

Yup.

"Whyy?!" She'd crawled into the secret hideaway again. "What are you doing?!"

"What? He can't see!" Wasn't like Nadia was about to reveal the whereabouts of any of her other secret hideaways to Visen and her blabbermouth…. "I'm just trying to figure out why he wouldn't want me in here if he isn't even using his office—"

The study's faux-ivory desk phone's missed message button came flashing red across Ivle's desk. "I bet you if anyone else calls it'll broadcast the message on speaker phone," —a standard perk, in case Ivle wanted to screen automatically whether or not he ought to be ignoring the caller.

Missed voicemails would just blare out, now, over that empty study, for no one to listen to, except maybe a wife secreted away behind her towel cabinet.

"No, he would've forwarded—"

But the phone, apparently, had been ringing off the hook; it started ringing again now.

'This is Evelle Ivle of Ivle & Ivle Incorporated I can't take your call right now please leave a message....'

Booop.

"Ivle. the Jolintans are wondering how we should apportion grain from the Care and Be Conscientious Initiative; can you call me?"

"He has control over who gets grain in Mertria's capitol?" seemed a bit like over kill.

"Yeah, see I told you his charities are a fucking nightmare—"

Another call came through.

Jesus Christ; how'd he ever get any work done?

"Eagle this is Bravo 3. Bravo 3 to Eagle. We have a transport carrier problem. Request storm troops. Over." *Beeep.*

"I thought you only ever said 'over' into walkie talkies,"

"I guess it works on phone messages too," Visen shrugged.

"Why not just text him?"

"This one'll be encrypted; easier to do with landlines,"

"Hm. Don't they know to call him at Frauzer?"

"Not—if he's avoiding further assassination attempts—!" Visen realized. "You're a genius."

"What? I didn't say anything,"

"Come on; get out of there—"

"Awwwh," Nadia wiggled out, all lingerie and curves, arabesquing up at Visen from where she crawled across the floor.

"Nadia..." Visen sat down, mind made up.

"Yeah?"

"Why did you tell me you and Badmonkof were meeting in the armory, and then go meet with him somewhere totally different?" Did it have anything to do with her continued persistence when it came to snooping around Ivle's professional affairs?

"Ah." Nadia'd mistakenly thought they were about to have sex again. "So. Me and Badmonkof usually met in that spare bedroom every weekend; I mean, it's not like Evelle ever sleeps with me in my own room anymore, but, y'know, safety in security, that sort of thing." Was 'safety in security' actually a phrase? "And I—just didn't want you to feel like you weren't special because I'd been seeing Badmonkof for—longer? Than we had been—? I mean, honestly, we were never seriously dating or whatever; you should've seen how completely and instantly his brain shut down the moment I opened my mouth to talk to him about anything. Anyway, I just—didn't want you to think we were that serious, so I pretended we didn't have a usual place to meet up. You ever, done that before?"

Being with Nadia was Visen's first romantic entanglement that had lasted longer than a week. She'd definitely never had to juggle two entanglements at once.

"I just wanted to make you feel special."

"Ok. Are you sure that's the only reason? Because, I don't care if we're on—different pages as far as, you know, sleeping together is concerned. But—that net was shaped just perfectly to fit you, and I just— need to know every possible detail you can think of that might help me know whatever the people who put it there are trying to do, right? Have you ever been—are you working for anyone?"

"No, I don't have a job."

"You're not maybe, passing on information to someone who might be able to use it against Ivle?"

"O-oh! No! Is that why you're so worried? Like quiet whenever Ivle's around?" No, that was just Visen's usual persona, mixed with fear of the power Ivle held over her. "Oh no, I swear I haven't gotten you caught up in anything nasty! Like I'm not trying to get secrets out of you! I just want secrets for the divorce papers; you wouldn't believe what's credible grounds for divorce; did you know, in Swiverlia, until 5 years ago, it was legal to divorce your wife on grounds she didn't cook enough?"

"Oh."

"So, I have to get some dirty stuff on him too, you know; do you believe me?"

Could she? That mouth slightly open like a fish, all absorbed in searching Visen's eyes with her own. What if Visen was the one coming up with conspiracy theories? It had been a very quiet few days.

"No, I believe you, alright. I just, got worried you were so interested in what he's been up to in that office,"

"That's because he has had like 62 liaisons with prostitutes and other mens' wives since I've been living here—62! And that's only the ones I've caught. And they've *all* started out in that office, because of the little secret entryway thing by the side." It wasn't entirely inconceivable Ivle had someone awaiting his return in that office right now. "I mean, do you think I'm not sexually satisfying?"

"No, it's, prolly just a power play."

"*Thank* you."

"Ok, but you do realize, don't you? If I fail at keeping you from exposing the secrets you find out by listening to— whatever's going on in that room—like with the voicemails and stuff—Ivle has every right to execute me—for failing to abate state espionage, because I'd technically be aiding and abetting if I wasn't preventing it. —Does that make sense?"

"What? No—you'd have to be court martialed before you're executed—"

"But I'm not working strictly within the parameters of the Mertrian—or—Swiverlian armies,"

"Wha—?"

"Right? This is just a private contracting job, so— please don't mention anything about that charity calling to anyone? Or the—weird, Bravo message with the transporters?"

"Got it. Oh my God, no, of course." They were silent a moment. "You're not part of the Mertrian army?"

"No, I'm a private contractor—for this type of job. I am also still part of the Mertrian army," for the time being, "but that's like—a second job." Come to think of it, most agencies other than OPSAI, wouldn't allow agents to just shoot one another through the head, the way she'd put Colby out of his misery. She supposed that was the horrific part of being a Bravo, always on the shady side of SEAL tactics. It was incredibly easy to make a Bravo simply disappear.

"So, he really did hire you to shut me up, then? If you're private?"

"Ah, no my main goal is to keep you from being kidnapped, but, he's indicated that it's—well, that it could be tied up with making sure you don't accidentally overhear something, and then, pass it on to someone else; like if you are kidnapped, and you know stuff, it'll make it so they'll have more leverage over Ivle that way, but, also, on a fundamental level, he just doesn't want you to get kidnapped you know?"

"Oh yeah sure."

"No, I'm serious!"

"I bet you he set this whole thing up, just to kill Badmonkof."

"But—okay, why would he kill Badmonkof if— like you were saying, Badmonkof's largely responsible for his respected position in politics? Y'know, with the—" Nadia sleeping with him to aid Ivle's career angle.

"Because Badmonkof *got* him the position in politics; you don't need someone once you've already gotten what they have to offer,"

Oh great. So— just how inappropriately *had* Visen fucked over her own country by agreeing to work for Ivle?

She tried to remind herself that Nadia was attempting to mash together grounds for divorce to take to the very lawyer Ivle'd be using to divorce her. She may have gotten a bit confused about the relative positioning of politicians' machinations too.

"I'm sorry I went back into the little hideaway."

"Mm? Oh no, it's—just please don't do it again, okay?" the awkward collide of professionalism and romance tugged worry through Visen's heart strings. She didn't want to hurt Nadia. Luckily, her face portrayed literally every facet of that turmoil.

"I tell you what, let's do something fun and crazy; so I can make it up to you!" Nadia didn't know all the worries that flooded Visen's decided inability to play poker face, but she was at least determined to make up for the ones she'd caused. "We can do anything you want! Ivle always lets me splurge when I'm alone—keeps me busy!"

"Even with your lover?"

"Well I mean it's also technically my money—like I inherited it and it went into the communal pot," she meant 'joint bank account.' "Besides, what he doesn't know won't hurt him; he probably thinks lesbian sex is hot anyway." Actually, he definitely thought lesbian sex was hot. He was constantly trying to arrange a threesome with Nadia and some other woman. Whether or not she was open to having threesomes was one of the first things Ivle asked when he met a woman. And by threesome he meant two women and himself. He wasn't about to have sex with another man (unless it was to bug Colby).

"You're sure we—I mean we should probably stay around here anyway; he didn't want you talking to anyone—"

"I won't talk to anyone. We're sitting ducks if we stay here and the kidnappers come back."

"Well—"

"We'll go somewhere safe and I won't talk to anyone! I mean like, you know, I'll be normal about it; but I won't mention things, y'know, that are in any way important!"

"Okay well I don't—"

"No that's what I'm gonna do! I'm gonna romance you! We've got three days," Nadia grew more and more excited at the thought and went to go put on a little black cocktail dress with asymmetrical wrap-around siding. "I'm very good at using credit cards you know," she looked over, self-consciously sly, "you go get lunch; I'm gonna think up a cool place to go for a girls' weekend out and see if we need to make an appointment!"

Chapter 31

Visen really didn't want to know what sort of day-spa they were heading towards, as Nadia bundled her eagerly into a waiting Rolls Royce.

But if anyone was still looking to kill Ivle, the use of his wife's credit card nowhere near Ivle's actual location might help throw them off the scent.

And it would keep Nadia preoccupied with things other than sneaking back to survey Ivle's top secret office.

Besides, Ivle's house itself wasn't exactly the impenetrable safeguard Visen'd once thought it to be.

So she had arranged for extra precautions when they went out, in the form of a mile-wide loose security perimeter, to surround wherever the car eventually took them.

As it turned out, they were chauffeured up to an industrial-chic building and left in the middle of an artfully rusted cement courtyard.

"Ok!" Nadia clapped her hands together. "I thought it'd be cool—and maybe you'd like to learn—…how to breath fire!" she did spirit fingers.

"Oh my God."

"It took me a while to come up with it because I had to look through your files first,"

Wait. The files locked in Ivle's study? God dammit she'd gone back in Ivle's study!

"It's like civilian flame throwers, but with your mouth!"

"You went in Ivle's study?!"

"No, I told you he has a little secret drawer behind his desk, by the exit,"

"Nadia—!" that counted as classified information!

"Oop. I mean, I haven't told anyone about it! Though…." Okay, starting again. Not blabbing secrets would be harder than Nadia'd thought. "I mean," she put on sultry eyes, "I just wanted to see what else you could do with that tongue of yours,"

"*Nadia...*"

The instructor was coming. *Fine. Just act casual.*

"You thought my mouth could use a little practice?"

"I thought you were so skilled I wanted to see what else you can do with it,"

The instructor arrived.

He exuded a vibe all ponytails and leather bracelets and the sort of carefree nonchalance that made Visen look, and feel, incredibly square and traditional.

"Alright, so what I want you to do, is suck the gas in with your mouth," he gave them a preliminary debriefing and exposition. "So, now, you try. Who wants to go first?" Nadia! Definitely.

"No, no don't inhale; don't inhale, just—hold the paraffin in your mouth,"

Maybe snorting gasoline wasn't the best activity to do with the woman whose life Visen'd been hired to protect?

Nadia almost gave herself permanent lung damage about 5 times. Eventually she settled down to just blowing a little tiny flame from her torch sideways repeatedly, via what may or may not have been simply exhaling without any extra fuel involved at all.

Visen got pretty good at it, though. It really was like that time she'd gotten splash-happy with the flame-thrower.

This was, actually, the best date Visen'd ever been on. Ever. This was amazing.

Nadia doubled down her efforts.

(Must reassure Visen their predilections were compatible).

"Oh, okay, no, no, okay—" the instructor was getting nervous again. "Don't swallow! Just, hold it, hold, in your mouth—"

"Sorry I'm just used to doing this sort of thing with water exercises—and penises," she whispered on the sly over the paraffin half filling her mouth, so only Visen could hear.

"Oh my God,"

"Ok ok ladies, ladies, no laughing; we have to concentrate; you're not taking this seriously enough—" that was about the fifth time he'd said that.

Nadia still thrilled at having made Visen laugh.

"Ok no now girls I'm serious: we can't do this properly, we're gonna have to sit this one out for a little while, okay?" He didn't say it very nicely.

Ugh, this was what was so irritating about being ex-military (—or, well, as good as). Everyone took Visen's capacity to retain humor during seriousness as a sign of immaturity. But that was only because they'd never been through hell themselves. Besides, it was only when Nadia actually concentrated on the task at hand that they were in danger of being blown to kingdom come, anyway.

"Hah! What about that?" Nadia rounded the vanishing wisp of a flame she'd spawned, like Russel Crowe's gladiator entering the colosseum, only for its wall of fire to just narrowly miss Visen with a loud hacking, spitting sound.

"Oh my gaw—sorry! Hah!"

"How'd you do that?"

Nadia had produced a sheet of flame, as opposed to the more usual arcing line.

"No no, that's a bit—maybe you should just sit it out a second—okay?"

"No no I got it! That was incredible!"

"Yeah, no, you've really—you've really gotta be a little more decentralized when it comes to the spraying motion, you're really not—"

"Look, I'm the one who's paying."

Right. Just, —the instructor sighed— she was also going to inadvertently kill herself.

"Uh, ok, you're just—ok, you're just puckering up a bit too much, here,"

"I think my lips are too fat—" Nadia'd already forgotten being angry that he'd managed to be so dismissively belittling at her height of triumphant flame blowing. This was way too much fun to hold grudges.

"No no, here, watch my lips, watch how they move," Nadia shot Visen a glance, thrilling at the fact her over-reacted 'ooh don't mind if I do' expression brought a grin, not jealousy, to Visen's face.

"Right." This was like those middle-aged cruise-line disembarkers in Cancun all over again. "So, what you wanna do—" the instructor tried demonstrating again.

Nadia produced another sheet of fire.

It was very difficult to concentrate with Visen just standing there all sexy, like a grinning goddess. Why did Nadia always get so distracted when she felt she needed to impress someone?

"Ok! Ok! I think I got it."

She spluttered again.

God, the flame dripped like, the entire length of her body; how was she even doing that?

"Ok, no you're not paying attention—"

Fair enough.

Nadia ended up just buying the pair of them expensive fire proofing suits, so they could practice at home.

"And 857$ is completely within my monthly budget," she promised. The monthly budget didn't get eaten up all that often, mainly because Nadia spent most of her time eating fruit.

"Oh, let me pay half it's my—"

"I'mma treat you," Nadia straightened up, eyes narrowed in faux warning: 'back away from the card reader.'

"Thank you…."

"And then the extra paraffin comes to an additional 875$…"

"Extra paraffin?"

"Yeah. I bought us starter torches too." (They'd been taught how to design their own as well). "With my own money; I have money too you know; I don't need to be a gold digger." They loaded all seventy pounds of explosive fuel into the back of Ivle's newly arrived spare Bentley.

"Wait I'm sorry what were you guys doing again?" the regular chauffeur had been supplanted by Wheeler.

"We were learning to breath fire,"

"It's a defensive tactic," Visen sat very tight lipped.

"Did you like it?" Nadia whispered from where she'd somehow managed to squinch, very petite and sensuous, into Visen's side.

"Yeah! it was so cool!"

Wheeler was sworn to secrecy. "You can't mention this to anyone,"

"I mean it'll be on the credit card bill,"

"Yeah but—"

"Just don't,"

Wheeler may only have been private paramilitary, but he knew better than to not take orders from a captain like Visen.

"I have cigarette lighters from when I was trying to quit smoking," Nadia remembered, as soon as they were back in her room,

"I saw you smoking like two days ago,"

"I've almost quit. Here, try these—" if they used the lighters instead of torches, breathing just a little paraffin allowed the plumes of flame to be indoor-sized.

They practiced Nadia's miniature fire-breathing tactic in her room until the pilot came to collect Visen to show her where Ivle's helicopter was kept. "Oh! Hello. Yes." Visen put away her lighter. "You're Piersfe, right? Do you have an ID?"

Chapter 32

"I'm sorry we're taking the precaution of flying ourselves," Visen explained as the pilot led her out to Ivle's chopper. "With the run ins we've had we believe one of the immediate household members may be a mole, so we can't take any chances,"

"Not at all; I understand," Piersfe didn't seem overly shifty. And the helicopter was in working order. No sneakily twisted bolts or tampered fuel valves (Visen checked). The tank was full.

"They've managed to update when the ceremony'll be. Ivle's hoping you'll be there by 10 am tomorrow morning."

"Wait what?" Nadia'd tagged along.

Frauzer was six hours by helicopter. Did Ivle habitually wake up at 3 am? Why was nobody else bothered by this?

Visen simply went ahead planning their route, receiving confirmation to fly while Nadia oversaw a maid service pack up her clothes and press Visen's dress uniform, which had been shipped over special: a Mertrian SEAL team kit, complete with Bonmount Acour medal, to impress as much as possible any Mertrians who happened to get close enough to notice her credentials.

Visen would wear fatigues until the last possible moment, then change into dress kit—or an actual dress, whatever the situation demanded. Moby Dick, and the rest of her gear—being in a state of constant readiness—were packed in an instant.

They both dozed from eight till about three in the morning, then headed off. Visen had found their best bet for gracious anonymity might be the Stules International Airport, about a thirty-minute drive from Hotel Buckensken.

No one arrived to greet them. The air was still crisp with early morning mist, as Visen called the habitual taxi service she had logged in her phone, amongst all the other non-committal numbers that kept snoopers from learning absolutely anything about who she actually was.

The taxi arrived. They bumped and jostled along in silence. Nadia was obviously sleepy, and the car had been too small to fit all her bags in the trunk, which meant they were now laid across Visen's legs.

The driver let them out along a low row of flags overhanging the beginnings of a morning in the capitol's central piazza.

"—Sorry," they were intercepted by a security guard at the Hotel Buckensken's front steps. "No one's allowed in at this time; the Mertrian president is making use of the facilities; I'm afraid I'm going to have to ask you to keep walking—"

"I'm here to see my husband?"

"The Mertrian president is dead—"

"Yeah well I'm sorry you can't—"

"Ms. Ivle!" a man in plain clothes came down to meet them.

"Oh!" Just who Nadia was suddenly clicked; the door guard'd seen her picture in the tabloids before. "Right; Ms. Ivle! Yes, right this way—"

"I'm her—bodyguard," Visen side-stepped awkwardly round him gesticulating to illustrate her relationship to Nadia like a crab to match her mood pre-morning-coffee. Her bid to slip by was successful.

"So, I thought the Mertrian president was dead?" Nadia called up after their escort as they rounded a third stairwell, Visen carrying all the luggage.

"Well—oh surely—? Ivle'll be inaugurated as interim president officially once he signs the papers after the gala this evening; we've just been making a few concessions in the late Badmonkof's name." Sounded a bit convoluted, legally. This must be one of Ivle's numberless lawyers, then. He did look very officially smug at the thought he wouldn't be able to explain it all to them.

They puffed finally into a blue sitting room marked 507, where Ivle sat flanked by thirteen additional advisors, seven of whom Visen had met in one capacity or another on the job, as equally blackmailed fish out of water, displaced from their own specialties to do jobs Ivle knew they couldn't refuse.

Odd way to build up a bodyguard, but Visen supposed Ivle always had been more on the political end of the spectrum, when it came to strategizing. Or had he gotten so good at paperwork he knew mounds of legal ramifications adequately protected him from anyone suddenly losing it and stabbing him in the back?

"Nadia." He nodded at the successful arrival of his wife, then beckoned her bodyguard closer: "she talk to anyone? Anything out of the ordinary? No unplanned trips?" he eyed Nadia, Visen following his gaze.

"No sir, one recreational, but I personally accompanied and set up a moving perimeter."

"Good. I don't want her fucking up public relations," he somehow got in even closer to whisper, "you see her talking to anyone you get in between her and them. Don't let 'em— she's fucking voracious— 'll sleep with anyone. And if she flirts with them, I look bad, yeah?"

Visen realized Ivle was simply picking up on the only way Nadia knew how to talk to people. Why, she'd even been flirting with that fiancée whose assassination attempt she'd been actively thwarting.

"Yes sir. I'll try."

"Good girl."

~*~

"You were right, then," Visen sidled back over to rejoin Nadia on the far side of the room, "interim presidency."

Nadia shrugged back a 'whoop whoop' in return.

Am I the only one who feels there's something weird about this? Visen didn't quite feel comfortable asking it out loud. Now she knew for sure this was no silly suspicion on her part, Ivle's ties to OPSAI somehow failed to reassure. But she didn't even quite feel comfortable admitting she felt anxious to herself, because she knew, as far as Ivle's bevy of lawyers were concerned, every law would be followed to the letter.

~*~

Their schedule, they learned, consisted of an inauguration, and then a gala, at which they could practice looking established in hopes people would be convinced to vote Ivle into office for a second term.

The gala would also serve as a chance to present Ivle with Mertria's highest peace time award, the Quadrivium, for having secured the safety of her people through steadfast dedication to initiating charitable organizations— "Oh my God! See I told you! Every fucking—! Whyyyy?" (Nadia). There would be a Slideshow presentation proving the power of coordinating international peacekeepers, as Ivle had done, when even the Swiverlian government itself took no interest in aiding Mertria. The reward served as a further hint that perhaps everyone ought to be ecstatically happy about the fortuitous turn in the tides of politics that led Ivle to Mertria's interim presidency.

Visen supposed 'coordinating with international peace-keeping associations' referred to installing the very Red Cross insurgents had told Colby they were so mutinously exasperated by, though of course, if this made Visen fear the gala promised to be a bit of a hypocritical bore, it proved nothing compared to prepping for the inauguration itself.

Nadia was forced to take off the nails she'd chosen specifically for the occasion, right after putting them on. "It's such a waste!" she practically stomped. They were almost four inches long.

"It's just a bit too flashy for the impression we're—"

"Oh, what? So I'm the whore now? Really? Sixty-two adulterous—"

"Vis-en."

It started as a calmly stated command but mutated very quickly towards the end into a whine for help. "See this is what

I'm talking about," Ivle twitched, "I don't want this—" especially now all his henchmen could hear.

"Not to mention all the—"

"Nadia, maybe we should—"

~*~

About ten minutes later they were all standing on stage for Ivle's inaugural address. The platform was horribly floodlit, even for Visen, who'd been trained to withstand ocular torture.

Of course, it helped nothing that she had to keep scanning the upper corners of the stadium for snipers—other than the sharp-shooters officially stationed by Swiverlia to out-sniper any unofficial snipers, should Mertrian insurgents start taking pot-shots.

As for the crowd, it was composed almost entirely of Swiverlians. Bit odd, considering this was Mertria's interim president's inauguration. But it wasn't like they could hide the fact practically no Mertrians had turned up. Different fashion; different genetics, on average....

Visen stood with her legs spread shoulder-width apart, hands behind her back, watching Nadia try her hardest to resist the temptation to slip her phone out, so she could play Blocker Blast—or whatever it was— discretely behind her handbag.

"Ahem," Visen cleared her throat noncommittally. Nadia's hand stopped inching through the opening between her purse clasps.

"Friends." Ivle started out, with a booming raise of both hands. "Federal Consular Legate. Sir Hosper, and fellow citizens. I am honored today to bring to your republic both condolences and assurance."

Nadia started picking at a blob of glue the rushed job on her nails had left to one side of her cuticle. Everyone else was watching the new interim president.

"At the untimely death of my predecessor, the Union of the Swiverlian Republics was under threat, not from external hardships or competition, but from the internal minutae of man's attempts to coordinate lasting peace. The strife that our armies and media have diligently and faithfully reported to our citizens is not to be mistaken as a sign of the necessity for war. Rather, it is an invitation to revisit our national differences, our habitual disputes, and our reservations when dealing with our brothers in autonomous regions other than our own." Damn, Ivle was pretty good, when it came to hiring out other people to ghost write his speeches for him.

"We Mertrians are a proud people, with traditions going back millennia. But in the past, we have aimed too closely to seek only the aid of those counted amongst our fellow countrymen."

Wait a minute—Ivle wasn't Mertrian. He was Swiv—okay. Nevermind. —Visen remembered just in time her poker face was practically non-existent. Not the time to be caught on national television obviously speculating on her boss' dubious duplicity. The glance she'd pulled too quickly to one side redirected itself into correctly bland, noncommittal, vigilant crowd-scanning.

"Today, we face a new world, and a new era. And while I am interim president, I will ensure Mertria does not close itself off from the benefits of collusion with her neighbors." (Everyone liked that.) "Nor will I allow those neighbors to ever over-run Mertria's natural self-sufficiency." The cheers were like a shock wave.

"To you standing with me here today, I promise that this interim government will strive to move forward to the peace Badmonkof strove to achieve.

"To our neighbors, and those in want and need throughout our Federation, we pledge our continued support and perseverance, to enable a meeting of the minds from all quarters of our Federation, bringing light where there is darkness, …restitution where there ought to be peace…."

Everyone stood to attention as he saluted the Swiverlian Asservation Committee dispatched to validate and confirm his inauguration. Everyone except for Nadia. She'd fallen asleep.

"Ahem."

"Oi."

She rose with all the humor of personifying one of the shadows under her eyes.

Chapter 33

They were led off stage shaking hands, in a round of congratulations which instantly failed to turn into non-committal conversation because Nadia was so very unlike all the usual middle-aged wives she'd known she wouldn't be able to imitate—as evidenced by her very vocally remembered "Oh yeah! Riiight," in response to the first politician's attempts at chatting, which stopped the entire room's buzzing for about half a second before everyone realized it was rude to stare.

After that it was only "Oh Ivle! And your lovely wife, aheh," as everyone nodded and shook Nadia's hand then instantly looked round for a more suitable discussion partner elsewhere. Nadia could sense a sort of nervous tension and started chewing her gum louder out of force of habit.

"Hey, hey yah nice to meet yah,"

"'chm, yes," the last terse little smile made its way back round to the hors d'oeuvres table and Nadia, for lack of anything better to do, fidgeted over that way as well, glancing back at the stoically frog-faced Visen, to make sure she'd tag along. "I don't like this," she whispered, once they were the only two huddled on the wrong side of the buffet. Nadia, unlike the rest of the ladies present, had a noticeable slouch when she had to wear heels.

"Me neither," Visen was just glad SEALs' dress uniforms came as Oxford flats and pants. Of course, the collar was still incredibly itchy. She glanced around for a second. "Am I the only one who feels like Swiverlia just took over Mertrian politics?"

"...Isn't that what they've always been trying to do?"

"Well yeah, but—" they weren't supposed to be so obvious about it. "No one's even saying anything—" it was like all the Mertrian politicians present had taken an oath to see a spade and call it fruit. Even the induction speaker had been rapturously excited to announce a new wave of broader Mertrian freedoms (especially when it came to commerce). —But it was the Swiverlians who'd always pushed for mutual trade agreements between Mertria and the rest of their Republics. Even if trade agreements really would benefit Mertria— they ran counter to what a thousand local politicians were continuously promising constituencies prior elections.

"I mean, the Swiverlians have traditionally wanted our land for like what the last 300 years now?" Visen confided barely audible murmurs over her sausage rolls. "And now we're just, what? Handing it over to them?" Ivle was Swiverlian, after all. Visen could believe Nadia's claim he was head of Secret Services to boot. She didn't mean to sound xenophobic; it was just she'd read about so many creeping coups that started out precisely this way.

"Yeah that's why I just don't talk about this stuff. Like somebody's confused it all the fuck up. It's like reading politics: you ever read politics? I keep reading and I'm like, this is a bunch of bullshit and this guy has a degree in it! Like every single point he makes is based on a buzzword he hasn't bothered to define so you can't tell if he's right or not 'cause you can't even define what he's talking about—so they never back themselves up with proofs is I guess what I'm saying; like they'll snowball this huge thing down into one little phrase and be like 'now here's what we'll do with this,' like they've got the whole world figured out but it's completely divorced from any reality. And then they think they're actually changing the course of history while history just goes on the way it would without them. Like, I would totally be a politician if the system actually allowed things to change. Instead, it's a bunch of people gossiping in a room and maybe once a generation they actually manage to pass a bill that's useful; and in the meantime, what? You kill yourself over handshakes,"

"So true," Visen was just trying not to grin when an admiral materialized searching for seconds and she had to turn her nod into a habitually formalized tilt of the head, in recognition of an incoming superior officer.

And then—she did recognize:

"Sir!"

"Visen!"

It was Corvan, Visen's old command leader.

He'd been promoted to admiral just about the time Ivle yanked Visen off active duty. "I'd heard you got transferred; how's the desk job holding up?"

"It's alright,"

"Did you get invited to the actual gala, you know, all the schmoozing?" Corvan put a finger to one side of his nose. That was the thing about Mertrians, you could instantly tell they were from Mertria; their mannerisms were goofier, somehow. It came as such a relief!

"No, I'm just here as body-guard, capacities...."

"Mm. Well, they won't even let me witness the president signing. Nope, straight back to my desk after this, right away!"

"Just new—" Visen pointed at his admiralty insignia.

"Oh yeah, just for show mainly—tell me, what do you think of it all?"

He sidled her aside, leaving Nadia hovering.

"Can a man who's not Mertrian still become president?" Visen'd been wanting to ask that all day.

"Yes, if he's adopted."

"Oh— that's clever." Must've been what Ivle'd been up to the past few days.

"I meant more how do you feel about the promise to revamp trade agreements?"

"Ah."

He'd completely shut Nadia out of the conversation by now, but come to think of it, Visen was bound by the specifics of her job to keep Nadia from entering it. She couldn't exactly just let her wander off, though— start up potentially incriminating conversations elsewhere—

God, she wished Ivle'd just deployed her to deal with those storm troops Bravo 3'd requested. That sounded so much easier.

There was a way, though, to include Nadia in their conversation with noncommittal eye contact and still return interest elsewhere in time to make sure she felt marginalized enough she never actually contributed. It was a nasty trick, but Visen had to keep it up. She couldn't think of any better tactic.

This was, in fact, utilizing the very sensitivity Visen'd always tried to hide from herself— knowing instinctively the subtle overtones in a room's atmosphere— being able to sense the peaks and troughs of Colby's interest, or of Ivle's surety in his own command. She'd always forced herself never to look past reality to those primary instincts that caused really nothing but a residual stain on the intent of conversations, the bits the unconscious mind within each party strived to conquer.

But now, she realized what power focusing on that subtlety could give.

It was perfect. Nadia stayed, eager to regain Visen's attention, while even Corvan grasped tighter for his sway over the conversation, at the subconscious realization it was Visen, now, who controlled their circle of three.

She'd been caught between two seekers after her attention before, making all the mistakes of imperfectly balanced attention, letting her eyes rest too long on one, feeling the minute affront of the other—all while they were meant to be discussing business, purely practical, impersonal matters.

Now she leveraged her attention between her two conversational partners on purpose.

It was such a nasty power move, wasn't it? But it was the quickest way to ensure Nadia remained preoccupied.

Visen would look in her direction, to invite speech, and then, in seeming carelessness, as soon as she opened her mouth, turn back to the admiral as though he had far more interesting things to say.

Regrettably, the newly minted admiral had just started in on discussing 'long term arms agreements,' and how they offered the opportunity to cement Livonian interests in Mertria, to bring stability between the two countries.

"That's why we need safe houses—safe houses," he kept saying.

Ivle, on a passing round, glanced at Visen just long enough to question if she was getting on alright with a raise of his brow. Visen nodded back; so far, so good.

"We protect the innocent with a new sense of interdependent consideration; it's sturdy,"—*how was Corvan still talking about this?* "It's economically advantageous, even, if we give the contract to the right contractor of course. So, what I'm thinking of wouldn't take away from Mertria's economic viability, when, say, other countries look in on us, because we would build up defenses mutually, in a mutual, long-term arms agreement— which is good for everyone in the Federation."

Honestly, it would probably have saved the world a few wars if Corvan'd just been wise and fearless and stupid enough to admit he just wanted to find a way to buy more Livonian guns without Livonia feeling they hadn't been properly compensated.

He might have even made a few good points in there, buried somewhere deep amid his repetitions, but it seemed someone'd taught him that if he did have something to say, he couldn't say it out loud.

The adjunct next to him, though, who'd seamlessly entered their conversation once he could be sure it included a bona fide admiral discussing arms agreements, was eating it all up anyway, while trying to get in a few buzzwords of his own, like "yes but the popular demographics—" which he must have interjected at least eighteen times.

It was around now that Visen began to realize Corvan was illustrating exactly what Nadia'd just been talking about. Maybe—Visen actually had leisure to speculate amidst the monologuing— all this babble was to keep people like the adjunct from holding anything Corvan said against him later, should it turn out to have been ill-informed. But it certainly seemed as though Corvan believed in whatever it was he was advising.

Just, how exactly *did* Corvan define 'mutual long-term arms agreements,' anyway? And then there was this 'economic viability.' He hadn't bothered to analyze the definition of that caveat any more than he'd bothered to analyze just precisely how long-term arms agreements wouldn't take anything away from it.

"So, we use safe houses to provoke a sense of security that can be used by communities to foster economic viability—" *ah-hah!* There it was again. "—while the arms deals aid an overall sense of interdependent consideration—"

"Wait, I'm sorry, what do you define as economic viability, again?"

Visen grinned.

Nadia'd gotten confused almost precisely where Visen had.

But the adjunct and Corvan looked at her like she didn't know what an economy was. "Well like, you know—the, ability to have healthy, wealthy citizens."

"Oh. Yeah, okay."

No fucking duh. What did they take her for? She'd *meant* what was the system—whether of freedoms or regulations—that the admiral was personally of the opinion would prove the most logical way to get to 'economic viability,' because if he didn't define what he was aiming for, they could never be sure whether the plans he supported would actually foster the end goal he sought.

But Corvan's answer was so insultingly stupid Nadia knew better than to assume it'd be worth trying to coax any more cohesive explanation out of him.

Visen, meanwhile, was beginning to have the uncomfortable feeling 'economic viability' was just a stand-in for not being quite sure which specifics of legislation ought to be analyzed when trying to determine what was and was not a healthy development for Mertria.

She could at least follow the rationale that Corvan's desire for 'interdependency' was probably a response to fears a pan-Federation economy would foist the burden of financing Mertrian administration on Livonia— which would, ironically, make it very unpopular to suggest any additional costs such as the safe houses Corvan seemed to be pushing—though whether these safe houses were to store the arms Livonia and Mertria would be mutually trading, or stood in for some sort of mutual outreach program aimed at facilitating citizens' safety in case of military emergency, Corvan hadn't quite clarified. But by now, his military position leading one to assume he'd meant the former, it would look impossibly stupid to attempt clarifying one's understanding by asking, to ensure he hadn't meant the latter.

Funny, how Nadia's estimation had been so entirely on point.

It struck Visen she ought not have been surprised Nadia was clever when it came to analyzing politics, rather she'd underestimated her simply because she came to them from a different point of view. A sort of soulless sexism, inherent in the state's politics, must have rubbed off on even Visen herself, she realized. There was always a time and a place to jump in and play the game, and say a spade was fruit, but if someone didn't get that vocabulary just right it seemed the world was all too quick to dismiss them, without actually listening to what it was they had to say. If you put in the right buzzwords, though, you could write a book and be considered expert.

Of course, no one would ever ask Nadia to elaborate on her ideas, as to how defining 'economic viability' might prove useful, because everyone assumed not knowing the vocabulary meant she didn't grasp the concepts. When really, from what Visen heard around her now, it seemed vocabulary stood in all too easily for any deeper understanding of the issues at hand.

It wasn't that Nadia was somehow smarter than Corvan. Visen knew Corvan; she liked Corvan— he was a good commander. It was just, she had an uncomfortable feeling that, rather like trying to explain the concepts behind Calculus, there were some people in this world who didn't know their subject well enough to vocalize it clearly, even to themselves. And Nadia was the only person in that entire room who'd admit the truth, that everyone there was most likely an expert on experts, but very few of them actually had any idea what it was they were actually doing.

After all, they were all groping after mass chaos. But no one ever paused to hear Nadia's point of view, for any length of time long enough to give Visen any cause for concern.

Chapter 34

Unfortunately, just as Visen began to realize there was something wrong with the way Corvan viewed politics, Nadia began to realize they were something wrong with the way Visen viewed her. The impression grew, each time Visen's roving gaze discouraged her from vocally joining in their conversation. She'd noticed as well, in the give and take, Visen's nod to Ivle, and to a mind used to ridicule, it seemed a covert recognition that she thought of Nadia as Ivle did.

Visen wasn't really interested in the dresses Nadia offered, as they got ready for the post-inauguration gala. She didn't really appreciate the tips to do her hair up nicely; she saw them as a curiosity to humor. And now, Nadia's mind began to pick, too, at the memory of Visen's response, when Nadia revealed the intimately guarded history that formed the core of how she always thought— "oh, that actually is quite insightful." 'Actually'? As opposed to what, exactly? What was to be expected? So it had been a slip of the tongue, did those not reveal more about underlying assumptions than anything else?

Nadia began to feel put out. And the more she tried to overcompensate by being obliging and eager, to help Visen into the right earrings, for a gala that necessitated she wear a long dress, the worse the feeling grew.

It helped nothing when Ivle stepped in, already dressed with the precision needed to make a good impression, four hours before he was slated to give his gala speech, to beckon, "Visen? Can I see you a moment?"

They left the room as Nadia was adjusting a final earring to make her neck look pretty.

Nope, no one noticed.

~*~

"Alright, I want you to make a list of the people my wife talks to tonight. Make sure she doesn't get into conversations about anything—" he equivocated in search of the right euphemism, "beyond her paygrade. You've got that?"

"Yes sir,"

"Then I know who I have to talk to, to do damage control afterwards; thank you."

Visen wondered vaguely if the names she'd report would be conflated with those weekly insurgency lists Desmond kept trying to steal.

"Just remember who they are; you can ask them, if you need to; that's your top priority for now."

Oh, for the joys of being able to make people disappear. Ivle went back to geling his hair. Unfortunately, the media'd already made far too great a mockery out of Nadia for her to simply vanish unnoticed. "Does that make sense?" He redirected attention away from the mirror to where Visen was still standing beside him. *Why?* She usually nodded as a way to excuse herself efficiently and took off.

"Yes sir." It made sense. "It's just I've never really run interference before this afternoon; I don't know how affective I can be once there's more people around she'll know, to talk to." 'Family friends' had been explicitly invited to the gala in large droves—gotta work those connections. "It's a bit easier when she's isolated,"

"Then keep her isolated,"

"Isn't that dangerous?"

"No, the kidnapping thing'll have blown over by now. As of the moment we stepped up on that platform this morning, Nadia has all the protections Swiverlia's political detail can enforce." And that division'd been protecting political spouses in semiautonomous republics for over 50 years now. Ivle just wanted Visen there to keep people away from his wife in general. "No, I just need you to see who she talks to, if anyone. Keep things light. You're still the one she trusts; the one she's comfortable around."

"Right." This was starting to sound like something that'd end in Nadia being permanently silenced. "I just—I don't really—I mean, I've been with her three weeks now, she hasn't really said anything—y'know—compromising."

Well, she had asked Nadia not to mention her conspiracy theories to anyone; Nadia'd know that included suspicions of planted nuclear power plants, right? Wasn't exactly a hard topic to keep out of normal conversation— Now Visen was beginning to worry. Just how far would Ivle go to silence his wife? "I don't think she really knows anything to tell." She just wanted to make sure... keep Nadia safe....

"Alright. Look. Smutt knew Colby was a carrier for my documents. Yeah? How'd anyone find out about that, hm? You know who knows that? The only person who knows who I call from, and into, my office? My wife. You know who she might've told about Colby? Literally anyone who comes within three feet of her."

"Right."

"And Visen? This is still just as serious as anything before; I don't care if kidnapping's out of the equation." Ivle was thinking of that Corvan fellow from the inauguration. He'd had to ask three underlings to snoop round before they finally found out that admiral's name—the difficulty of procuring such a reasonable little request for information was what had inspired him to think maybe he should order Visen to just keep a list in the first place. Best put Corvan on that list too, once Visen brought it in. "You just keep her from talking. You've got it?"

"Yes sir."

Ivle could tell her attitude had changed.

Visen could tell he needed reassuring.

"It'll be fine; I'm sure."

"Are you kidding?" he glanced back up from combing in final applications of mousse, to where—he'd suddenly realized— Visen stood looking stunning in Nadia's fashion sensibilities.

"I just meant it's—probably not the time or place—for her to bring up anything confidential; since it's just a celebration. It'll be—fine," *Oh no*— Visen slunk back into professionalism; why did over-familiarity with Nadia have to translate into unwarranted freshness with her boss?

"*Are* you kidding? She's surrounded by politicians; it's the perfect opportunity for her to make a fool out of me,"

"You think she'd do it on purpose?"

"She's a nasty bitch Visen; she'll do it just for the attention. You should know that by now."

Oh. Okay. "Yes sir."

~*~

Visen spent the next few hours worrying how on earth she was meant to keep a mental catalogue of every person Nadia spoke to. Would it be too obvious to write it all down in a notepad? Did Ivle really trust Nadia so little?

It certainly made for an awkward ride over, at any rate, to the state department where Ivle's gala would presage the official, private signing ceremony at 9 pm that'd make him president: Visen, trying to be respectfully professional, despite the fact Nadia insisted she wear a singularly well-tailored evening gown; Ivle, pointedly only looking at his phone; Nadia, trying to analyze the atmosphere between them.

"Alright, good luck," Ivle cast back one last raised eyebrow over a curtly lipped nod at Visen, before diving out into the audience surrounding their car.

That was it. Nadia wasn't blind. That was the 7th time they'd made eye contact about her. With each other.

She pulled Visen aside as soon as they left the Rolls Royce; Ivle, naturally, having been swept inside instantaneously by cajolery.

"Look, are you after my husband?"

"What?"

"You're trying to angle me out, aren't you? You're after my husband!"

"What?!"

"You think you're smarter than me, you think you're better at politics—'ooh Nadia those nails are too long;' 'don't slouch during the inauguration!'"

"What?! No! I had to back up my boss! I don't care about your nails!"

"Oh yeah right. I see you guys eyeing each other, y'know; and then all the sudden you're all awkward around me; I know what you're up to—all those goings and comings and those secret little whispers right in front of me you guys think I won't notice; and the phone calls. I tried to keep you interested in my side of it—but no he's the new president; I'm just some tart who can't keep from fidgeting on stage—"

"You think I'm cheating on you with Ivle?"

Bravo 2 was, after all, one of the original reasons Nadia'd made that hidden panel to spy on Ivle's office in the first place.

"'Oh, that's so clever you think about politics,'" Visen could just tell from the falsetto, this was a direct quote of what Nadia's memory had warped recollection into making Visen say. "Yeah, I think about politics; if you really thought I was so clever why didn't you let me talk to that captain Corvan, huh? Do you not trust me? 'Cause I promised I wouldn't say anything controversial! And I've been doing a good job!"

Their pause by the car was beginning to feel conspicuous.

"We should probably—"

"No. We're gonna talk about this right now."

Oh my God. Nadia really was kind of —needy, when it came to wanting attention.

"Nadia-a!"

"What?"

Visen glanced round quickly, wondering how long the limo could excuse their presence before reporters began to suspect they hadn't simply paused to grab something out of its trunk.

"You really don't trust me, do you?" Nadia squinted. "'Cause I promised! I wouldn't say anything controversial! But as soon as you have Mr. Corvan—oh no no don't let Nadia talk! Or have you spent this entire time thinking I'm so stupid you can sneak around with Evelle right under my nose, and the fact you won't let me talk as soon as you have some fancy-pants Captain to impress is just another symptom of that underlying truth?"

"Um."

Someone took a picture of them.

"Corvan's actually an admiral now,"

"That doesn't make any difference!"

"No, it does! I can't just—it's not socially acceptable to be like 'hey, here's my friend I'm introducing you to now' when it's an admiral; I'm only a captain; captains just kinda, you know, nod along to whatever admirals have to say—I felt weird; I'm sorry—did that—that really bothered you that much?"

"Uh, yeah, that and the fact you've been eye-fucking my husband all night!" she didn't want to add, 'and he's been eyeing you back.'

"What?!"

"I see you two,"

"I'm a—bodyguard! I'm looking to make sure he doesn't need to tell me any new orders; he's just telling me what to do—"

"Oh yeah sure, by looking at your ass,"

"You're the one who dressed me up!"

"Yeah well at least he has business meetings with *you*, doesn't he? For no reason. Every two seconds. As soon as you have a dress on." That actually was an oddly fair point, but surely Ivle had better options to choose from—?

"We were just discussing what we need to do with you,"

"And I'm not even allowed to be there?"

"No; you don't need to be there; I'm the military defense strategist!"

Nadia sulked. She had a bit of a problem. She'd always let herself be pushed and pushed before she realized she was actually upset. Then, she'd have to act more upset than she actually was, so people would notice. Otherwise, she'd forget she was upset, and people would continue walking right on over her. She was simply so used to mirroring what people expected to see from her, she never knew when to admit to the outside world that she felt everyone was being mean to her.

She went to go pout purposefully, over by the catering stand, rum punch in one hand.

Oh my God, really? Nadia was so stupid! And she'd worn those four-inch nails Ivle'd told her people would find gauche, just to prove a point.

Visen actually kind of liked that. If she ever found four-inch nails were the only way to express herself, she'd probably have worn them too.

But being the target of Nadia's pout made Visen feel as though Ivle had a point, as well. Why so suddenly jealous? Did she *have* to match so accurately every single stereotype of an ignorant housewife? Nadia was cool, but, also, kind of... weird. Or, ill mannered? Was that a class difference?

Probably the difference between being drilled constantly in the military and— what? Marrying rich? Never having known mental discipline since high school?

Absolutely unfair; Nadia was very smart. Just— kind of stupid. Or, it struck Visen at the moment, very sad. Whatever she hadn't meant to do had hurt Nadia. Really, she supposed, if two people she herself cared about kept making eye contact at her expense all night, she'd probably feel a bit left out too.

But that in itself wouldn't illicit such a desperate, almost panicked quickening of sensibility.

—Suppose she really had been looking for an opportunity to discredit Ivle, leak what she claimed to be state secrets on purpose? Could that explain why she cared so much no one let her immerse herself in the very milieu she had only a few minutes previous discounted as overwrought Byzantium?

But that was just doofy Ivle paranoia.

No, it was more than that; it hit Visen like a guilty memory of what she'd known all along to be true. No, the worst of it was this pout meant Nadia thought she was losing the husband she depended on, if not for money, to maintain the status quo to which she'd grown accustomed—and pouting was the only means at her disposal she could think of, by which to gain power over his attention again.

That clawing over-reaction meant something defiantly defeated— which Visen had until this moment taken to be immaturity— slunk through the bounds of Nadia's self-defining fear. Such a little fear too— hoping to keep some power over a husband meant to be her equal and going about doing so in all the wrong ways, equating insolence with self-expression and trying to maintain it as a comfort in the very ways she went about defeating herself— such a little fear, compared to the shifting concern with which Visen kept a look out for snipers. But who was she to believe that when the time came, the panicked adrenaline of searching for shooters was somehow more deeply cogent in its connection to the human condition than the everyday malaise of waiting for a divorce? Hadn't Visen always wanted to go out quickly, with a bullet to the brain?

No, Visen's own lack of care over the wounds of socializing, the snobby 'more suffering than thou' attitude with which she would have viewed Nadia's ridiculous pout, all this was simply the result of having gotten so used to being brainlessly downtrodden by the professional hell of a work-place culture that thrived on the necessity of everlasting subtle bullying.

It was like when the US tracked down the Boston Marathon Bomber. Visen'd been stationed over there at the time. All that antagonism, such seriousness—she'd looked on it with scorn, as nothing but the workings of a spoiled elitism, to be so hell-bent on revenging so minor an infraction of their joy. Did they not know hundreds of Mertrians were bombed to death every year?

It was only when she visited Pearl Harbor that she'd realized what had happened.

The little sheep mill of a presentation playing tragic violins to vows of 'never again,' 'never forget.' For what? 200 soldiers? 3 million people had died in the war that slogan's retribution spawned—but then her better self surprised its own intuition, as it sometimes did, by wondering when she'd begun to count 200 people as too low a number to mourn. No, it wasn't spoiled, even to mourn the death of 1 runner, to try to ensure it never happened again—that was an attitude all the world ought to have the right to be able to share.

It was just, to see those she blamed, in part, for her own country's suffering—if for no other reason than the weight of their sheer ignorance—

Still, the old train of thought that she'd met at Pearl Harbor passed through Visen's mind as one iota of a second's vision, like half-remembered dreams.

Alright, she'd go try to be nice to Nadia, even if she was being stupid and pouty.

Chapter 35

Visen had an idea as to what they could talk about, at least. If Ivle's inauguration ushered in all the protections Swiverlia's secret service could enforce, Visen didn't need to worry about mentioning that little hidey-hole Nadia had in her bathroom anymore, in an attempt to strike up conversation. Both the Ivles had far more efficient safeguards, now.

But if Nadia wanted to feel respected— Visen did respect her; she just needed to show it.

"Hey, Nadia?"

"Hey." Over-dramatic raised eyebrows, then a shift away. Honestly? Such a 12-year-old. Jesus.

"I was wondering…" Must remain calm. Visen tried to make it as obvious as possible she was attempting amelioration. "You know that hiding spot—in your bathroom?"

"What?"

"The—safety room you built, behind the towel cabinet in your bathroom?"

"The what?" Nadia hissed as though trying to bite Visen's words back into her face.

"What?" Why'd she look so betrayed? Visen'd just confided enough suspicions of Swiverlian duplicity to get herself killed over pigs in blankets a few hours ago. No one was listening to them. "It's just—" she channeled all the seriousness of talking to an admiral, "you know the safe-houses Corvan was mentioning? Well, they reminded me a lot of your saferoom, and I was thinking, maybe, in the future, y'know, Mertria could use some of the insights from your design. So, like, y'know—the—concept."

Hopefully Nadia'd pick up on the fact they were discussing tactics, just like Visen had with Corvan.

But there was only silence.

"So. …What was your thought process? Y'know, behind making it?"

"What do you mean?"

"Like, why'd you decide to build it… the way you did?"

"So in case someone wanted to kill us we could hide?"

What'd Visen think she'd built it for?

Had she picked up on the fact its sole purpose was to spy on Ivle?

"Right, so it was designed as more of a safe room, or more of a—look out?" Visen was genuinely interested in that one.

Oh, so she did know it was meant to spy on Ivle.

"I dunno; Ivle just kinda does iffy things legally, I guess, I just figured if anything ever blew up, I wanted to be safe."

Oh *good*. So Visen had been the one to start up a conversation with the capacity to compromise Ivle.

Good thing Nadia'd decided to pout so far away from all the other guests.

"No, no I meant like—uhm —like why not get, y'know, like—an—actual saferoom?" with metal sides.

"What do you mean? It is an actual saferoom."

"No, I know." Did Nadia know what a saferoom was? "Just—And, you, decided on a—panel behind the towel cupboard, 'cause—"

"Because that's what Corrie Ten Boom did. She's my hero. It's the only safehouse I've ever heard of that actually worked."

Oh. That actually did make sense, didn't it? Germans walked right past it.

"It doesn't disturb the layout of the house, so people don't know there's anything there to look for."

Visen's brain buckled under the weight of having underestimated someone in the very way she went about telling herself not to underestimate them. Stupid dumbass… —of course even housewives dreamed of thwarting Nazis.

She opened her mouth to respond, but Nadia'd already caught on.

No more being cajoled back into friendliness. She wasn't that dumb. She idled away, under the pretense of swirling through social clusters like the rest of the party goers.

Chapter 36

Galas were where Nadia had expected to feel the most at home, as an interim president's wife. She'd worn a floor length gown and spent approximately five hours making sure her face looked perfect, only to find the artistic effort wasted on balding councilmen and their wives who took her for a hussy. She hadn't been dressing up for their husbands! She'd thought she'd finally fit in! She thought galas were meant to be parties, not lukewarm dinner plates.

She picked at her fancy pasta sourly.

By now, Visen was tired from a day of being constantly on the lookout for superiors she had to nod to.

She was lucky Nadia's natural loudness did away with any need to actively keep her from talking with others. Politicians preferred steering clear, and Visen had only to trail about two meters behind Nadia, ensuring no more than polite pleasantries were exchanged. Surely Ivle wouldn't want her to take down the names of every passing person who nodded hello.

But as the gala's official dinner started, Visen was getting jumpy at memories of Badmonkof's memorial luncheon.

The gala itself took place in a sort of funnel of a hallway, down the length of which ran two arched colonnades, front-lit, so that the darkness beyond, which led outdoors, could host any number of kidnappers or assassins without betraying a shadow.

It felt very, very open.

Visen realized the ability to mill around between social clusters had actually functioned as her security blanket. Now, Nadia was literally a sitting duck, set to one side of the main dignitaries table that stretched the width of the hallway's far end.

She sat, at least, perpendicular to the direction in which all heads had now turned —to watch a video promoting Ivle's recent charity work —the hope seemed to be that if people were saps enough to come watch him receive an award for his charity, they might be willing to give money to the charity being applauded.

If anyone did hustle in with a meshy body bag, Visen supposed 300 witnesses would at least probably cause enough chaos she'd have time to intervene.

She tried to relax, keep from over-taxing herself with hyper-vigilance. Nadia was Swiverlian Security's problem now; and they'd do a much better job at protecting her than Visen alone ever could, if she could trust Ivle not to have staged this whole thing for some nefarious reason all of his own.

Half of her did fear he'd simply told security to just go ahead and shoot his wife—the military half that was used to analyzing every possible contingency.

Visen wouldn't exactly put it past Swiverlian politics.

But her other half calmed her into trusting the everyday humdrum of a society in which unwanted people were strategically spirited away at night, open assassinations were frowned upon, and the jumpy perfection of a combat soldier used to ducking unseen marksmen may have just been overkill. She had to trust government more than that. This was just a function.

"Nadia?" Visen whispered, craning her neck to one side so the chair wouldn't squeak as much as she leaned imperceptibly. No response. Oh, come on! You could hear a pin drop, if it weren't for the presentation, they'd been shunted so far off to one corner again, compared to the rest of the guests. "Nadia!"

"Yeah?"

Way too obviously still purposefully ignoring....

"I'm sorry I didn't let you know about what Ivle and I were planning for your security."

The way she said it didn't sound passive aggressive, at least.

"You're right, you should've been there for it. And when we exchanged eye contact, Ivle really was just checking in."

Visen obviously hadn't spent much time analyzing the ulterior motivations of men who liked to whisper in the ears of women wearing plunged necklines.

"He made me promise to make sure I recorded everyone we talk to, so he can make sure he talks to them later and there aren't any misunderstandings. I told him you'd promised not to mention anything compromising. He just didn't trust me to be able to keep you from doing that, since none of us really know what might be compromising and what might not be. So it's not that either of us mistrust you or think you understand the situation any less than us. He just wanted to make extra sure for the night before he's inaugurated, since there has been some question of kidnapping you for information, that none of whatever that information is might be leaked at all. That's why we kept signaling and going off to discuss stuff; he was just checking I was ready to try to get the names of everyone we talk to.

"—And you're right we should have included you in the discussions; I don't know why I didn't. Like maybe I thought it would hurt your feelings somehow because it's basically telling you not to talk about certain things? But it's actually a lot better that you're in on this too; you can help me remember who we talk to; I don't know what I was thinking."

"Okay."

Nadia still sounded pissed, but slightly less so.

They continued watching the presentation in silence.

Turned out she hadn't been joking about the soccer balls.

There was literally footage of happy children playing soccer.

"*In the upper reaches of Northern Mertria,*" a soothing voiceover melodiated, "*Nigel Cormash rarely goes a day with access to clean water,*"

Visen forced herself to relax again, lulled by the mediocre video presentation.

"*He came in one day, and he said to me, he said,*" —a little blurb at the bottom of the screen announced they were watching a project-site manager discuss how Ivle had changed her life, *"this is unacceptable, this needs to change. And he really did change things."*

Turned out Ivle had provided 82 villages with fresh drinking water over the past two years alone. Visen's interior conception of her own self-consciousness, which at times personified itself as her, in cartoon form, scrunched down into its own little mimic of the gala's folding chairs, in horror at its own villainy. *Hooray!* For sleeping with the wife of a guy who'd saved thousands of lives. This felt great!

"Over the course of 5 years, the Covilen Institute has transformed this once barren desert into an oasis of culture. Infrastructure, community centers, and programs for Women Becoming Entrepreneurs, with full scholarships for over five thousand and seven..." oh jeez. Odd how personal and public lives could clash so forcibly. Visen hadn't known the man who actively discouraged his wife from any pursuits more vocal than Basher Blocks could be a feminist. Or was it only that Nadia had sucked in sexism too? Could she have done something with her life, underwritten by Ivle? Maybe both had simply stopped talking after a while, assumed the worst in one another, so Ivle saw no hypocrisy in his private life, because, to him, it was Nadia who was being lazy and unproactive.

Didn't really help that he was so constantly dismissive of her, though. That'd be enough to make anyone feel worthless.

"...making universal health care the norm for Northern Mertria..."

What if—could Ivle have been right to blackmail Visen about the amphetamines? Maybe he *was* just doing his patriotic best, ensuring what he defined as justice but—with mercy. It had been a nice arrangement, not to let anyone find out. A bit old school... was Visen herself another charity case?

She was beginning to think she ought to give more credit to whoever was in charge of this presentation's propagandistic overtones. Mediocre video-presentation indeed....

"...This extensive new healthcare infrastructure stretches from new ambulance fleets to state-of-the-art facilities, especially in need amidst the war-torn regions of growing insurgency activity on our northern Livonian border, where this 18,000 square foot enclosure—"

—Wait a minute, where was this, again?

Visen had recognized one of the hospitals.

It was *the* hospital. The hospital that still came to her in dreams sometimes; where she'd won her Bonmount Acour. Eight stories high, set in a shrubby desert on all four sides. There were mountains in the distance. It was beige, and they'd tried to mellow the brutalist architecture with shiny white edging round all the windows, which always, in her memory, amidst the blinding sunlight, made the windows look dark and receding, like little pits into a soul.

Visen's team had been stationed about five kilometers away, tracking binoculars over the routes potential smugglers could take, to watch for insurgents. Some of her men had been in that hospital. On the third floor, when the alarm went off.

Pipes running through its walls had suddenly heated to boiling, vaporized steam pouring from the roof. Electrical lines had caught fire—

Visen had been trying to read Proust's *In Search of Lost Time*, for a lazy Sunday afternoon, in her field tent.

She remembered the scramble; the smell of burnt plastic—

"Captain! Cap— the hospital!" The hospital itself was on fire, by the time all stations had scrambled.

They'd been warned this could happen. That hospital ran on two tons of highly efficient transductive energy, an experimental model that could only go drastically wrong should temperatures rise above 2000 degrees Fahrenheit. They'd always known fire could pose a risk—so the hospital had been constructed with new fancy-ass synthetic materials, that could burn hotter than thermite but helped, so the Mertrians had been told, with ventilation. The place had been blanketed with enough dampers that even if fire broke out in over half the building, it could easily be contained; the heat wouldn't travel.

Now, though, it certainly looked like the heat was traveling.

"Scramble! Rogers! 2 6 over; all teams to base hut now!" Visen's walkie talkie had connected to the base's temporarily rigged loudspeaker system. (This was Mertria after all. Again, not the most sophisticated, when it came to technology.)

By the time they'd billowed troop carriers across the five kilometers of desert between them and the fire, a small, spindly ladder had been attached to another small, spindly ladder, on top of which two men with buckets were tossing water sideways onto the flames.

The buckets were then relayed back down to the rest of Mertria's official regional firefighters, who'd formed a chain.

"Get the hose!" Luckily, Visen's regiment had been equipped with countermeasures precisely in case something like this did happen—one couldn't trust insurgents to spare anyone these days, even hospitals. And the way the fire had spread so efficiently—no one really had any doubts insurgents were ultimately to blame.

But their quartermaster had only sanctioned Visen's base with two hoses. And both of them were tiny.

She had watched the smoke rise up into the third floor. "Give me a mask! Sevran, Walitz, suit up! We're going in!"

During the next 48 hours, they'd evacuated every floor. Visen's lungs would never be the same (you expected Mertrian masks to be dependably airtight?).

It turned out the experimental fire-retardant construction materials did a great job of welding doors shut, though they were legitimately successful at segmenting the fire off to keep patients relatively safe, just— trapped behind emergency exit door handles reaching temperatures of about 380 degrees. To be fair, that was considerably cooler than the temperature at which the rest of the building was burning.

They had carried the injured and ill back over the plains, towards their own orderly's back up medic's lab, fumbling oxygen tanks, calling for extra ventilator masks, surgeons, tissue reconstruction for the burn victims.

No one came to relieve them.

At least the building had held.

By the middle of the second day, though, Visen had had no choice—extra amphetamines, to keep her alert through the night, as they scoured to clear what had been the most ambitious of health facilities, now, a death trap to inch through, groping along the walls with sensors in an attempt to preemptively detect the built up pressures bomb squad assumed were what had to be responsible for repeatedly ripping out whole walls, right when responders were most ready to help evacuees.

If Visen hadn't had her amphetamines, she would've been too tired to think to use the army's regulation mine-sweeping devices, in the hopes that whatever was causing wires to explode might register, to these poor, metallic saps of outmoded Mertrian technology, as the same built-up electricity by which they identified the hidden positions of mines. It had worked.

And then, by the end of the second evening, 9pm, she'd had to call it: "We have thirty minutes before those Croffes explode; get your men out of here!" She remembered clear as day, for some odd reason, how a wisp of her hair had blown over one side of her face, as she hollered at the startled fire chief.

"Croffes?"

"Power supply! The power supply goes off if it reaches 3000; leave now; we can't save the building!"

"Is everyone out?"

That question still haunted Visen's dreams, long after she'd been awarded her medal.

That question, and the fact that, when they'd surveyed the wreckage for damage, they found thermal sensors laid into the hospital's foundation. Not, as might be expected, designed to serve as a forewarning should Croffes grow too hot, in fact, quite the opposite.

The way they were wired, the sensors wrapped round to every single hospital bed; there wasn't an electrical inspector who could have missed them. They even impaired the foundation itself somewhat, the way they displaced pipes. But plumbing, and inspectors called in to greenlight the foundation's initial pour, found absolutely nothing to worry about, according to their reports.

Which was a pity, because, it turned out, when the heat those sensors picked up from sick and injured patients reached a proper pitch, i.e., when those who had placed them could be sure the hospital was fully operational, the sensors had been programmed to trip a switch, connecting each sensor to one of 86,000 small detonators, all minuscule enough they would never have been found, had Visen's inspired use of mine sweepers not prompted the Mertrian army to call in experts to investigate, with some idea of what it was they were searching for.

They never told the public that part of the story—untraceable detonators would have caused too much mass panic. The news'd already caused mass panic enough amongst government officials; they'd been horrified insurgents had access to such advanced weaponry, especially when subsequent covert operations had confirmed the wiring couldn't have come from illicit Livonian help; the Livonians didn't have any technology that advanced either.

They never did learn how Mertrian revolutionaries got ahold of such advanced explosives.

Law courts condemned all seven of the inspectors who'd okayed the building's continued construction for having accepted bribes, paid off by insurgents to look the other way.

But as for who had actually planted the bombs, they hadn't a clue. Mertrians had a habit of decentralizing documents, by housing each set of official records in the public buildings to which they pertained. They thought it was safer that way. So of course, all records of who helped lay that foundation had gone up in smoke. They'd known a few contractors, but never to trace it all back as far as Ivle, all the paperwork on silent partners, third party consultants, and less noticeable affiliations had been destroyed.

Of course, ever since Visen'd been employed by Ivle, she'd known he controlled thermal innovations almost exclusively; it was why she knew to hope they could survive in Nadia's uninsulated safe room.

It was thermal sensitivity that had triggered the charges, that day.

But she'd never before thought to connect Ivle with the hospital that had exploded.

And now, here was Ivle's self-promoting presentation, proudly proclaiming he'd been the one to build that hospital.

Of course, for the Swiverlians who made Ivle's presentation, it was just one of many lovely hospitals Ivle's charities had helped erect. But at the time, it had been the only hospital in Mertria that was functional. Families had been camped in stairwells, to provide dinner and clean bedding. And Visen had been in charge.

—Come to think of it, that'd probably been the operation that alerted Ivle to her use of amphetamines. It was certainly the only time Visen had proven so flagrantly incautious when it came to disguising her dosing routine. In fact, she couldn't think of another instance in her career that would have displayed infallible energy enough to warrant an investigation into its origins....

She supposed it would take several subsidiary charities and hired out independent contractors to complete a hospital's foundation. Suppose Ivle's charity had accidentally hired Mertrian insurgents? That wouldn't look very good for Ivle, were

Visen ever to decide to engage in a little counter-blackmail. Of course, that would mean she was piggy-backing on the destructive violence of murderous terrorists, but....

"Ivle & Ivle Incorporated now partners with the Red Cross to ensure our investors more than due diligence when it comes to responsible charitable spending.

"With the Eveitson Project, every new charity that comes under the umbrella of the Red Cross' aid distribution undergoes a comprehensive and thorough background screening, to ensure no money is funneled to insurgencies or home-grown terrorism."

Right. —And there went Visen's hopes for counter-blackmail.

Seemed a team of 'international consultation lawyers' had taken care of any possible potential for Ivle to be linked to anything but sweetness and light.

The video glided down a spreadsheet of dozens of charitable recipients, chairmen and organizations listed in seeming perpetuity: post offices, public service contractors, dental associations, every single Mertrian school district's superintendent (there were only 8 school districts, but still)....

Not a single Mertrian name on that list.

Huh. Yeah that was a way to keep out insurgents. Make sure you never gave money to anyone from the country that needed revolution.

Chapter 37

The lights finally flickered back on, for final (30-minute-long) speeches about how funding creates opportunity. Then everyone was finally free to start milling round the buffet while Ivle & Ivle Incorporated hosted a silent auction for bids on paintings made by victims of a North Mertrian burn unit, brought in after insurgency strikes. All proceeds went to Ivle's charities, of course.

"Nadia? Can you help me figure something out?" They were still sitting shoulder to shoulder. Neither had any interest in strolling over to see the interactive art exhibit one lucky bidder would get to take home.

"Nadia?"

"What?"

Visen's continuous whispering was beginning to feel like barraging Nadia's feelings down into forgiveness with nothing but persistency.

"I need to check the names on that spreadsheet they showed in the video—the list of charities Ivle's contributed to, along with their owners. Do you have any idea who else would have a copy of that list?"

"Yeah, Badmonkof did; it was in his little 'I'm gonna blackmail people with this stuff' section in his briefcase,"

"You took it?"

"I ripped it up just in case. It didn't seem very important to me,"

"Do you know anyone else who might have a copy? Is there anyone who helps Ivle make business decisions?" Visen would bet anything there was a copy back in Ivle's locked study.

"I dunno; he has a different lawyer for every country he does business with,"

"So who's his lawyer for Mertria?"

"Jacobsan,"

"Oh, yeah yeah,"

"Yeah the guy we go sailing with sometimes," Nadia hated sailing, almost as much as she hated golf— somehow Visen didn't seem interested.

"Can you introduce me to him sometime?"

"Yeah sure." Nadia stood.

"Whu—?"

"He's right over there," lounging in a room hung with maps off to one side of the main gala's dining hall.

"Oh. Alright, awesome. Just uh, ask if we can see the complete list of charities I guess; right? Like we're just— interested? That works right?"

"Yeah that works,"

"And don't tell him anything Ivle wouldn't want you to tell him—like, you know, anything with the kidnappings or anything okay?"

"What? I'm not gonna say anything!"

"Yeah; perfect; we'll just be light and breezy,"

"Seriously? You think you should be the one giving me social etiquette perimeters?"

"No, remember that's what I was saying—"

"If Jacobsan wants to kidnap me we're not telling him anything new; if he doesn't he can help us—"

"Yeah but it might jeopardize or destabilize—something; I'm sorry; I realize it's stupid. It's just, Ivle didn't want us, you know—" spouting off information to every single person in the room. "It's just my job,"

"Yeah that's what everyone always says."

Was that a veiled reference to the Corrie Ten Boom thing?

"We just don't know who could be listening in!"

Nadia hautied over, Visen internally calculating how refusing to tell a family friend about family matters may not have been the hill she should've chosen to die on.

"Hey, Jacobsan?"

"Nadia!"

"Do you have a list of those charities it showed Ivle donated to?"

"Hm? Yeah, they're by the door,"

"Oh,"

It was obvious neither Nadia nor Visen had noticed that. Jacobsan thought it a bit airy of them, especially for a bodyguard. Visen went to collect one of the pamphlets, skimming down as she walked back. No—she'd been right: not a single Mertrian name.

And it wasn't like it was that hard to notice.

50 years ago, the Mertrian president at the time (a man named Even Marcle of Snykes), had mandated every Mertrian take up a corollary to their last name, to differentiate them from Livonian and Swiverlian neighbors. It would allow Mertrians to finally process paperwork using surnames, instead of epithets like 'of Snykes' to ensure they didn't confuse their own president with Livonians who shared the patronymic 'Marcle.'

The Livonians, of course, had already switched to using last names long ago, at almost exactly the same time Swiverlia did, which meant they'd managed to take all the good ones.

There simply weren't very many names available in the offshoot of bastardized Hungarian-Slavic their three countries shared.

The corollary Mertrians were forced to take up proved to be an addendum of either '-an', '-itz', '-sfe', or 'ka'— or 'ze'—which one you got depended on which region your family currently inhabited. There were only ten different regions in Mertria, so it was incredibly easy to recognize the corollaries, or, in this case, the absolute lack of them.

And it wasn't simply a matter of Swiverlians transcribing cultural quirks into their own, more codified understanding of how last names ought to work, either, because the '-an's '-itz's and '-sfe's didn't just go at the end of last names. Sometimes they went in the middle, or at the beginning, or as a penultimate syllable (Mertrian names could get awfully long).

Visen double checked twice anyway: not a single '-an's, '-itz's or '-sfe's to be found. Of course, there weren't. No other country would be stupid enough to implement a set of only 8 addendums. Of course— as soon as this self-deprecating thought crossed Visen's mind, a simultaneous and overwhelmingly indignant patriotism rose up as well: So Mertrians were stupid; they were her stupid people, dammit!

Now what was it that so frightened Visen about the fact no Mertrians were given charity?

Was it not that this was exactly what the insurgents had claimed, that night Colby riled them into complaining, while masquerading as a Livonian soldiers?

'The Red Cross is stealing our infrastructure!'

"The Red Cross is stealing our jobs!"

Visen, like everyone else, had assumed that was just a lie superiors told subordinates to ensure compliancy.

Oh sure, give them cause, give them cause— manufacture a sense of vengeance, and ensure they feel no guilt associating with an organization so obviously responsible for the very deaths they claim to be avenging.

But what if superiors really did believe they hadn't been the ones to blow up that hospital?

Well, Visen supposed, then that would mean someone was trying to frame them for bombing the hospital.

But who would benefit from framing insurgents?

Unless it was the very charity which, even now, had spent the last ten minutes proselytizing how it would continue to maintain order by controlling bureaucracy, "till peace regains the region."

Would certainly tally with what Nadia claimed about Ivle's underhanded backdoors and smuggled documents.

But that was insane. You didn't give 50,000 people drinking water just to take over a country—although, Visen supposed, wouldn't exactly be the worst way to go about doing it.

Come to think of it, the dried, monochrome sentences by which officials relayed to headquarters the heroics that had garnered her a Bonmount Acour could never on their own have given Ivle the impression she may have been using amphetamines. He—or whoever had reported to him— would have had to see her eager alertness, to tell there was something off about it. To know for sure. But there was no reason for a civil contractor or Swiverlian secret police to post surveillance on a hospital that'd been erected months earlier—unless they were waiting for something.

No, no, no. But surely— Ivle must've simply been monitoring Livonian-Mertrian border crossings, under the banner of OPSAI.

But then why replicate the very task Visen's team had been sent to accomplish?

Odd, how it really did all come down to a question of vocabulary.

Visen had been willing to smuggle USBs, to masquerade as a Livonian aid to insurgents, because all along she'd known OPSAI was a legitimate organization Swiverlia had set up to foster Mertria's peaceful realignment into semi-autonomy. What if…? It was simply a pity she'd never bothered to ask what OPSAI meant by 'regional peace' beyond vague assurances of altruism.

Was this what it meant to see a spade and call it fruit?

Were blown up hospitals considered as necessary as shooting Bravos, so they wouldn't talk?

And all the charities that had control over infrastructure in Mertria were of foreign origin.

Hadn't Nadia always said Ivle's charities weren't actually designed to help anyone?

If Ivle had exacerbated tensions by blowing up that hospital, if the Mertrian insurgents had been right, even if only on that one point alone, then this wasn't an interim presidency, this was an invasion.

And Ivle'd taken the head office of their state in the same way he'd taken their roads and postal services, as an act of charity.

~*~

Of course, there was one person in the room who'd never bothered to claim Ivle 'fostered diplomatic relationships with discussion;' who never claimed he 'facilitated partnerships to further inter-state cooperation'— who just came straight out and said he'd made a subordinate insert blueprints into Mertrian archives, for Livonians to find, that falsely insinuated Mertrians had nuclear capacities.

—No wonder Swiverlia could claim it was necessary to install their own head of secret services as interim president, if Mertrians seemed to be hiding nukes from their neighbors.

What was it Nadia had said that first night, over cucumber soup? It'd all been done to keep Livonia and Mertria frightened.

That made sense. Wouldn't fear result in precisely what Swiverlia, Ivle's charities, and OPSAI had all along promised to achieve? If people were terrified of insurgents, amalgamation would feel better than destabilization. Then, there'd be no more wars between Livonia and Mertria— not if Mertria had ceased to exist. No more fears of 'training exercises,' if Swiverlia unofficially incorporated Mertria, under a puppet government headed by their secret services. No more cross-border sabotage. Nothing left to worry about except why OPSAI categorized exploding hospitals as strategically necessary for stabilizing a region.

Only now, it seemed someone had finally taken an interest in what it was that Nadia had to say, hadn't they? Not Corvan, not the adjunct—but that man in the frogman suit; the search and sweep—it hadn't been by twos, had it? That'd always bothered Visen. Standard offensive procedure required a search and sweep in pairs.

But what if the search and sweep had only been to ensure safety in a low threat environment by setting up a defensive perimeter? Like the kind used to guard a meeting? That only required single-cell guard operations.

Supposing there had been two different parties out to catch Nadia, and one, the man in the frog suit, had just come to talk?

Even Wheeler had sensed Ivle wasn't worried for Nadia's safety. He'd hired Visen because he'd been worried about his own.

Because if whoever had come that day, slipping through Ivle's study in a frog suit, could get Nadia to talk— they'd find Swiverlia, or at least the man Swiverlia trusted to be in charge of Mertria, had been behind Mertrian-Livonian antagonism all along.

Chapter 38

Suddenly, it no longer seemed so profoundly important that no one find out about Visen's amphetamine usage. In fact, she was embarrassed blackmail had ameliorated her into excusing away suspicions of Ivle's nefariousness for so long.

Nadia had Swiverlian state security to look after her.

Visen needed to go tell someone what she'd guessed—warn someone at least, before Ivle's official signing into presidency. No one else knew as much about Ivle's machinations as she did; no one else could match Aplidexs—to say nothing of exploding hospitals— to the fact Nadia might be telling the truth.

"Nadia? I'll be right back, okay?"

Nadia'd been sucked into a conversation about how much Jacobsan enjoyed golfing with Ivle four Saturdays ago.

"Yeah take your time," she tried to smile.

Visen flipped round the map room's exit and dived for the nearest private hideaway. A bank of five payphone booths still tallied along one side of the state department's marbled entryway, providing much-maligned privacy for state pensioners, despite the landlines themselves having long since vanished in the wake of cellphones.

Visen had decided to call Corvan. He'd said something about being needed back at his office by the time the gala rolled round. She simply wished she could use something less hackable than her cell phone. Of course, knowing Swiverlia, the remnants of landlines she stood by had probably at one time hosted the most monitored phone calls in all of Eur-Asia.

Didn't matter if Ivle discovered she'd called Corvan, she supposed, not now.

Stupid Mertrians always had fought tooth and nail for independence. Stubborn, idealistic little twats; the thought got

Visen grinning a mercurial grimace determined to overcome patriots' tears.

She knew an old number, comprised of only three digits, that connected straight back to the telephone relay service at Corvan's command base. They'd given it out to all Mertrian SEAL captains three years back. She could only hope it still worked.

It did. At least, a voice on the other end of the line answered her call with a single, coded salutation: "Transponder."

Ivle's 'Eagle' code had been based on Mertrian military protocol. Only, in this protocol, Visen was 'Jerry 6', not 'Bravo 2.'

"Jerry 6 speaking I need to contact Ishmael,"

"He's at canteen at the moment; can I take a message?"

What the—? It was 9 o'clock at night. Was 'canteen' code for something?

"No, I need to speak to him personally; can you get him on the phone at once?"

The operator jostled off. Command base— even Mertria's central headquarters— wasn't exactly big enough to encapsulate different departments. Everyone knew everyone. The facilities mainly took the form of a large, interconnected bunker.

"He'll be here soon," the operator finally returned.

Visen waited, twirling at the string that still attached a disused phone book below the metallic shelf framing sockets from the old ripped out landline.

Suppose Ivle had staged the intended kidnapping? It could explain how Wheeler managed to drive the intruders out so fast and why they'd been released from the local constabulary. Ivle himself could have been the one to lay the trap for Badmonkof. In the form of a trap that looked like it'd been set for his wife. Of course, she'd never be able to prove it either way— she'd never be able to prove anything— unless they could get their hands on those documents in the secret compartment only Nadia knew—

"Sir!" she heard Corvan pick up on the other end of the line.

"Jerry 6?"

"I have information regarding Mertria's new interim president,"

"If it's the fact he's Swiverlian secret service, we've already had 86 civilians call it in,"

Wow. That— okay.

"No." She decided to start at the beginning, from the first suspicion she could pinpoint by name—the Aplidex. "I'm calling concerning the border security Ivle recently installed. I have some proofs and suspicions which, if further corroborated by action I hope to convince you to take, may necessitate a subpoena rescinding Ivle's ability to take office."

"Jerry, you're going awful fast—"

"I have to go fast sir; my absence might be noted—" She didn't want Ivle to come barging in, interrupting.

"Weren't you assigned desk duties—?" Corvan must not have realized she was still at the gala.

"Yes sir, please listen. I haven't had time to formulate a persuasive argument, but I can present certain facts to you."

"Okay. Shoot,"

"Alright. Concerning the border security Ivle recently installed for Mertria: he included a backdoor by which others with the right access software could infiltrate the Mertrian system. I believe he sold that backdoor to Livonia. I know, because I was the one who delivered the necessary software to Livonia. I watched the cyberattack take place. I just didn't realize until now what it was that I was watching.

"Now, Ivle's wife is the one who made me suspect this might be what I saw. She reports overhearing a conversation in which Ivle planned to plant proof Mertria has been developing nuclear arms on Mertrian systems for Livonia to find, presumably during this cyber-attack. If you get in touch with a certain Johann Smutt, he will be able to provide you with information handed over to him by a man whose name I knew as Colby Briant—he may have been using an alias. That man was shot moments after he delivered information to Smutt, but I believe, whatever that information was, it must corroborate Ivle's wife's claim that Ivle has been playing Livonia and Mertria off one another."

"Ah—ah no Jerry we already know about this; Colby was planted by Livonia to discredit Ivle,"

"But Livonia *did* find plans for a nuclear reactor in Mertria's databases; a reactor that didn't exist,"

"Again, that was Livonia—"

"No, those plans came from Ivle. His wife saw him hand—"

"No, no—Jerry. All plans must have a physical copy to instigate and maintain the electronic sister copies as per Mertrian software protocols—not just rules; it only works if you have a physical copy; we checked. Ivle had no physical copy,"

"But I know where he hid it."

"It's impossible; we had the best teams—" Corvan ranked high enough to know all about Badmonkof's search of Ivle's properties.

"No. Once those teams left—and I was there sir—Ivle's wife said that they had failed to find a hidden compartment in Ivle's desk where he stores his most secret documents. I don't know where that compartment is exactly, but I know it should be 'behind' his desk; that's what she said; I'm assuming that means on the side of his desk that faces his locked study's side exit—there are two studies. I would suggest raiding that locked study, in particular, again." She gave Corvan the address of the particular vacation home to which she was referring.

Proof of her amphetamine usage would be in there too, most likely. But, in fact, what embarrassed her most now was the fact its discovery would prove she'd believed blackmail could come from a viable strand of government. She'd simply been brought up with dysfunctional nepotism, part of a system half bought through by bribes for long enough she'd assumed OPSAI's political maneuverings could all be part of some larger government plan to keep the peace. But if those plans involved blowing up a hospital—

"There's more. A charity by the name of the Covilen Institute, working directly under Ivle, may be responsible for the destruction of —— Hospital 3 years ago, on October 1st. At the time we found evidence of a thermal triggered bombing system. If we analyze those remains, which ought still to be held in evidence for five years according to our statutes—" and if those remnants hadn't been retained something fishy was afoot— "we may find proof linking the bombing to Ivle's own thermal devices. No one ever knew where those bombs came from because they didn't think to link the institute that made that hospital to Ivle's other businesses, which manufacture thermal sensors just like those found at the scene of the fire."

"That doesn't prove a link to Ivle,"

"It does if that particular technology was at the time unknown to any other corporation than Ivle's, which I'm betting is the case. We have the patent dates; the research and development paperwork will be in his office."

"It could've been someone else at the company, maybe this Colby."

Ah, shit. She'd have to tell him everything.

"No sir, Ivle himself seems to have been in charge of many different measures that were taken to pit Livonia and Mertria against one another. For example, I can personally testify that Livonian munitions runs to Mertrian insurgents were infiltrated by team members including myself and Colby, on Ivle's orders."

"On Iv—?"

"Directly from Ivle. At the time, I thought we were infiltrating munitions runs to help Livonia catch pro-insurgent citizens from their own country. But now, I think Ivle used subordinates disguised as Livonians —as both Colby and myself were disguised— to make Mertrians think Livonians were helping Mertrian insurgents, when really, there were no Livonian insurgency sympathizers to begin with. We did catch people during that operation who did look like they came from Livonia, helping Mertrian insurgents, because they were in Livonian military garb. But I was one of them. I was instructed to pass myself off as a Livonian, and Ivle freed us all later. So, if I was one of the Livonian insurgents; what if all the rest were only claiming to be Livonian, too?

I think we can prove the entire thing may have been staged, by tracing the connections between those arrested as Livonians that night and Ivle.

"Again, I can testify that Ivle himself tasked me with delivering the USB I believe was used to crack Mertria's defensive network codes. I took a USB to a Livonian embassy in Mertria the night before Livonia's cyberattacks on Mertria. I have reason to believe that was not a coincidence. The man I talked to mentioned feeding information that USB allowed him to access back through a software—or hardware? —called an Aplidex.

"Ivle's wife corroborates this claim, saying Ivle handed a USB over to underlings that was capable of breaching Mertrian cyber defenses. The timing of when she saw this USB corresponds to the time at which I was tasked with delivering a USB. They have to be one and the same. If you can find out what an Aplidex is we should be able to prove that Ivle was behind the Mertrian data breech.

"His wife is the key to proving my suspicions; I've been tasked for the past three weeks with the job of keeping her silent under pretext of worrying about her safety. But I think Ivle's not worried she'll be kidnapped; he's worried she'll talk, the way she did to me. We need to take her down to the cardel"—a main government interrogation center in Mertria— "as soon as possible; in the meantime, I've told you the gist of what she knows.

"Uh. You realize if this is true it's more of a government concern—"

"I don't know who in the government is working with Ivle or Swiverlia. I chose to trust you because I know information Ivle has been withholding from you, personally, which makes me believe, once you know it, you may at least be able to— personally— realize there is something wrong with the way he conducts business."

"What information?"

"Regarding the use of illegal amphetamines by members of your old task force."

"What?"

"The fact he chose to keep this from you should arouse some suspicion, at least, of his transparency."

"You're saying he's been running drugs to my men?"

"No sir. The amphetamines were prescribed, simply used against army orders."

"By who?"

"By me. It's how he blackmailed me into working for him. He claimed he'd tell you, if I didn't run certain 'errands' for him. Errands including those I've just enumerated."

"Then—why are you telling me this now?"

"So you'll believe me when I say Ivle is up to something. I wouldn't admit to this if I wasn't convinced my fears can be proven and indicate a dangerous enough situation it's worth risking—well, everything, for me. If you can subpoena a warrant to search Ivle's house at 66 Cleveland Drive in Mertria, you will find a locked study with documentation, and voice message recordings, to confirm everything that I say, that there is something funny about the way he conducts charitable bureaucracy. I'm worried his involvement in the hospital explosion—"

"Unproven,"

"—if proven, insinuates his use of charities to bolster Mertrian economics has been corrupted to further his own agenda."

"And you're sure this uuh—USB, isn't just some Swiverlian tactical maneuver? Sanctioned to maintain the status quo—keep the peace?"

"That's what I always thought it was sir. That's why I haven't reported until now. I still think it might be instigated by higher Swiverlian government. But if it is, sir, it's closing in on Mertrian autonomy in a way that's not legally binding as per our Constitution—if for no other reason than that blowing up a hospital and bypassing our defensive networks is no legitimate mechanism by which to maintain a balance of power!"

"So you're turning tail, is what you're telling me?"

"Yes sir."

"I think this is more for the associated press, maybe—"

"Do you believe me that we may have cause to fear Ivle's claims to interim presidency may lie on a backing of carefully orchestrated duplicity? In which case, regardless of who is orchestrating duplicity, it may prove detrimental to our country's freedoms in the future." The Swiverlians had, after all, been hoping to expand into Mertria—and Livonia— for the past 300 years.

"I don't know if—maybe—this sort of leveraging is fairly common—"

"I know sir; blowing up hospitals isn't."

"I don't think we can pin that on him—"

"If we can't pin that on him, we should be able to pin something on him. Go to his home study. He's hidden somewhere in that study paperwork that corroborates his involvement in planting the false Mertrian nuclear power plant; like you just said, he has to have the original copies.

"I can give you the names of 6—no, 5" —(Colby was dead)— "other individuals who, like me, have been blackmailed into doing Ivle's dirty work. They should be able to corroborate, if anything, at least my movements the night of September 20th, the night Livonia breached Mertrian cyber security." She gave descriptions of Max, and the housewife whose party she had slipped through.

She was glad she'd used the emergency call-in number; there was no way Corvan'd listen to all this babble for so long otherwise. Huzzah for procedure—it alone ensured her access to power; sad how such a hated thing alone gave her validity.

"We just need to get a search warrant,"

"I don't—think it'd be wise so soon after inauguration to show such open hostility—"

"Sir, I'm saying I can prove Ivle orchestrated international escalation; we should hold off on the inauguration—"

"Well it's a bit late—"

"He doesn't sign off until 9 pm tonight."

"Oh?"

It was a new ceremonial precaution.

"I don't think we've got enough to go on—"

"What about the fact Badmonkof was mysteriously murdered in his house? I can give eyewitness testimony—"

"'ll, but—they caught the fellow who did that!" Smutt had told Corvan it was a fellow named Connor Jacobs.

"What? Who?"

"Mm some lower level bureaucrat—"

"How'd he do it?"

"Slashed him across with a knife I think."

"That's impossible; whoever killed Badmonkof used a triggered pulley system to strike a chord across the hall right as he walked by."

"Oh." That hadn't been in the official report. Corvan shuffled desk papers idly. "Well, um. Like I said I feel like the sort of leveraging you're describing is fairly common—"

"But I can give you three separate suggestions of above-and-beyond nefarious actions Ivle has taken that we can pin on him, if you find those people I've just mentioned." She knew the address of the housewife. Max would be easy to trace through his job. "At the very least we can show he resorts to blackmail,"

"Mm…" Corvan asked for her to repeat the names she'd rattled off.

"And if you procure a warrant to search his study and take apart his desk you will find paperwork that proves what I'm saying—very possibly the original documents that, like you said sir, the Mertrian government originally felt it necessary to search for, simply without avail,"

"Well we can't get a warrant for that in depth an operation for at least another—"

Oh lord. "Ok, yes. I think we may be able to alert others to the fact there's cause for concern, though? That could at least stall Ivle's being signed into presidency until we get our hands on more evidence,"

"Right, but do you have any proof to alert people with, beside your own testimony?"

"Yes. I've just found proof that Ivle's charities, at least, the charities under his control, have been systematically denying Mertrians services from Red Cross subsidies. If you take a look at a paper I can give you—that's been handed out to every guest at tonight's gala—listing those who have received aid from Ivle's umbrella NGO, you will see infrastructure contracts have been routinely rewarded, with implicit Swiverlian approval, to Swiverlians and other nationals of foreign origin within Mertria. There's not a single Mertrian name on that list. Now I know there's an international treaty—"

"The Fitz-Patrick Sanctionings, yes." The Fitz-Patrick Sanctionings required 50% of charitable cashflow inserted into any semi-autonomous Republic to be aimed at invigorating the business and finance of citizens belonging to that republic. "Eh, You can get around that, technically, though, if you say that, technically, since it's infrastructure—"

"Yes, sir alright, I understand but what about the implication that he's blackmailed me? And what his wife says? Now I'm just saying we can hold off the inauguration ceremony with those concerns—we can use the Fitz-Patrick Sanctionings as a delay— but the real damning evidence comes from his wife,"

"Isn't his wife trying to divorce him?"

"Opposite way around,"

"Still makes for an unreliable witness…"

"What about me, sir? As a witness? I was ordered to shoot dead a man named Colby Briant, at Ivle's command. Now, he claimed this was all done under the auspices of OPSAI. I believed him; I didn't want to make a fuss. But if you're saying later claims allege Colby was nothing more than a plant to frame Ivle, my testimony can disprove those claims."

"I mean they'll say this was all just a Swiverlian tactical exercise?"

Oh God….

"Just. Do you believe me, that we may have cause to fear the claims Ivle secured inter-Republic peace may have been orchestrated? So, regardless of what they were orchestrated for— that may be some cause for concern?"

"I mean I'm sure they were orchestrated."

Of course, Corvan'd known all along Ivle was Swiverlian Secret Service masquerading as civil contractor; that was a non-issue; he'd been brought up under the same bureaucratic clusterfuck of bribed nepotism as Visen had.

"Well if that orchestration involves blowing up hospitals, assassinating Mertrians like Colby, I think we can safely assume Ivle may prove detrimental to this country's freedoms— in the future." *How many times had she said that?*

"But I only have your word to go on."

"We just need his wife to show us where additional secreted paperwork is that can be used to condemn Ivle! And I can get her to do that. How long would it take to procure a warrant?"

"A couple of days at best; but Ivle has full rights to strike down that sort of search once he's president. On grounds it's a matter of national security."

How had that ever been allowed into their constitution?

"Alright then, I'll delay him." With the Fitz-Patrick shit. Or all of it. She'd just pore out her confessions to the seven or so Mertrian generals who needed to sign declarations to make Ivle's presidency valid. "Can you get a search warrant by tomorrow morning?" Visen could keep the signatory committee talking all night. Just needed to take some amphetamines....

"Okay. Jerry 6?"

"Yes sir."

"I'm gonna go out on a limb and try this. But I want you to know I'm only trusting you because of that Bonmount Medallion you won. I respect that. But if we don't find anything, this falls on you."

"Yes sir."

"I'll call you to let you know a warrant has been served. Don't pick up in public. It should take about five hours but it'll be a few hours after that before we can get a chance to get into Ivle's." The security systems on these secret service mens' mansions were universally known as atrocious to try to bypass.

"Thank you, sir," Visen rang off.

Now, to stall Ivle's being signed into presidency.

Chapter 39

Honestly, Visen had never noticed it so poignantly before, but she had enough of an inferiority complex to sincerely believe it was possible she'd simply made all this up in paranoia.

But no one could live knowing they hadn't tried to stop injustice. It was like prisoner's dilemma for conspiracy theorists. Even if there was only a 1% chance Visen was right, the gravity of what she could stop by coming forward outweighed the gravity of the 99% plausibility she'd simply look insane. So, she dived forward on the off chance.

She had a plan, kind of.

By the time she returned to the gala, Ivle & Ivle's silent auction was still running; Ivle himself was standing at the back of one colonnade, surrounded by what appeared to be sycophants peppering him with polite laughter before his signing ceremony began at 9.

That signing ceremony needed seven generals, representing all government subsections, including civilian, to make the inaugural covenant binding. If Visen could explain her fears to the Mertrian members of the signing party, at least some of them might back down in good faith. If all this turned out to be overactive conspiracy mongering, she was due for a court martial anyway; at the very least being recorded as testimonial at court might spur side investigations that could lend credence to her claims.

Most of the Mertrian signatories could be picked out from among the auction's audience by their ridiculously ostrich-plume themed military decorations. Visen scanned the crowded rows from behind. She could see only their backs, but from the shoulder lapels she counted 3 senior Mertrian officers, and five others of high enough military rank to be considered government officials.

"Visen! Why are you not with my wife?"

Oh shit. She needed to buy time.

"I've lost her sir. I'm getting help as we speak,"

"What?"

"I left her in the map room with your lawyer Jacobsan; they've since disappeared; you double check the map room; I'm calling in favors I owe—"

"What the—!"

"Please double check sir. I may be wrong. They may have gone to another room and we simply missed one another; I'll have Mertrian higher ups handle this in no time without making a scene; sir—check. You know her better than me,"

"Absolutely—ridiculous—" Ivle huffed, loping, off to the map room.

Visen bent beside the nearest high-up Mertrian official. "Sir? I'm SWAT team commander 7; I need you to come with me; I have a matter of national security to discuss; can you alert," she nodded her head towards another bidding general, "and meet me at the back of the room? I don't want to cause any alarm." She did that to about five more officers she could be sure had stood in Mertrian ranks long enough that probability, at least, favored their being loyal to the Republic. If one of them was under the sway of Swirvelia, she could count on some trickily executed death, for even attempting to admonish Ivle, but at least they would all hear what she had to say first.

She had just finished explaining her concerns with the promise of documents to prove her claims by the following morning (assuming Corvan pushed his search warrant through), when Ivle reappeared.

"Why the hell did you stop guarding her? Where is she?"

"She's not in the map room?"

"No."

"Oh." Well fuck. "You know, I think I made a mistake; I think I actually last saw her in the yellow room—"

"She's not in there either. I checked. She's not anywhere. And Jacobsan's missing too; you were right."

"I'm sorry has something happened?" the nearest general's personal decorum bridled at the thought of being left out of a conversation.

"My wife is missing,"

"O-oh," ruffles of disconcertion derailed national concerns to sympathize with personal ones. "—perhaps she went to bed early?"

"No, she's not in our rooms," Ivle's nostrils were flailing enough from suppressed panting to confirm he'd probably run there to check.

"Mm." the Mertrian officers looked to Visen, to see how she'd interpret.

"Check the CCTV monitors; they're bound to pick her up somewhere,"

"I did! How do you think I know she's not in any of those rooms? She's gone Visen! What did you do with my wife?"

Chapter 40

It was Visen's turn to eye the generals uncomfortably.

At least this could delay the signing ceremony?

Good thing Visen was even now and very quickly utterly repudiating all prior highhanded decisions she might actually be on the same side as whoever wanted to 'talk' to Nadia. Seriously, who goes to an innocent tête-à-tête in a frogman suit?

Visen no longer trusted these people.

Where the fuck was Nadia?

"I'm sorry," one of the generals sensed she'd stalled, "We were just discussing matters of national security, sir; if you could just step away, for a moment—"

"I outrank all of you,"

"Well—"

"My wife has just been kidnapped!"

"Right. Yes. Well, I mean— I'm sure she's probably just gone for a drink; let's—" About half the generals grouped round Visen now tried moving as one to draw Ivle subtly aside so the rest could keep talking.

"No!" Ivle hissed his elbow out of the nearest's friendly steerage. "Don't you think you can— conglomerate without— president—"

"Sir, you're still a civilian contractor until you sign that inaugural—" one of the senior officers, at least, seemed to have bought into Visen's claims.

"I am SMD of the Swiverlian SP," (SP stood for secret police; SMD was its head.) "Now what the fuck did you do with my wife?!"

Ivle glared at Visen. He'd never suspected Visen before. Just what was she playing at? Revenge? A delaying tactic? To keep— from signing—? Had he just caught on to what these Mertrians were trying to discuss?

"I'm sure she's safe,"

"She's not safe; she's been kidnapped; you idiot!"

Though, knowing Nadia, she could have just gone for a walk to ogle Swiverlians.

"Have you tried calling her sir?"

"Yes of course! She never answers does she?"

Visen tried again, just in case, hoping she looked like she was just humoring Ivle to get rid of him, and was not in fact in any way unnecessarily distracted from vital matters of national security, despite probability practically ensuring Nadia's safety. She had the Swiverlian secret police guarding her; Ivle didn't want her gone, she wouldn't be. And Visen doubted even Ivle was skilled enough at acting to pull off this reaction as a pretense.

She tried to calm her adrenaline into staying focused, waiting through the ringing. No answer. She tried texting instead. Better wait on that one a few minutes, though, if breakfast with Nadia had taught Visen anything, it'd only take Ivle's wife a few minutes to respond. Nadia had a very robust texting addiction.

"Sir I do need to talk with these men, for just one moment in confidence, please,"

"No! You engineered this didn't you? I saw you duck into that bank of telephones to call someone!"

"What?!—"

"You kidnapped my wife!"

Oh, for fucks sake—

Now the entire charity gala had turned round to stare at Visen.

The bank of seven Mertrian generals began subtly trying to move to one side, in an attempt to sweep Ivle into an unobtrusive side corridor.

"No! Don't you—!"

"I'm sure it's just—"

"Don't touch me! You—!"

"I didn't have anything to do with—"

"Then why are you—?"

"Look, I'm in the middle of explaining to these men how you seem to have sold a way to infiltrate Mertria's new security systems to Livonia, and then may have planted documents to make it look like Mertria was planning to nuke Livonia."

"Oh—Colby—are you kidding me?"

"Your wife is the least of my concerns at the moment! You told me I was off the hook soon as you gave your inaugural speech!"

"Look Badmonkof already dealt with this; it's slander—"

"They're been new developments,"

"Like planning to kidnap my wife to delay the inaugural—?"

"We're currently discussing how to proceed prior to arrest and legal negotiations against you, so please, stand down! Your wife is fine!"

Ivle's jaw dropped. He might as well have mouthed "fuck you."

"Also, if you could hand over your phone for the time being, sir—" One of the generals grew wise to the fact whatever papers might prove Visen's claims could be highly flammable. "Now would be a good time to act in good faith, if you hope to prove your innocence later."

Ivle's jaw snapped back shut.

"I'm not handing over my phone!"

"Then make sure he doesn't call anyone with it," Visen nodded to the colonel to her left to delegate specifically. "—Good thought. —Not that it'll do you any good to contact anyone," she added for Ivle, "we already have documents corroborating—"

"Like hell you do," Ivle whipped out the phone he'd defensively pocketed and started texting menacingly.

But one of the older, grumpier generals swatted it away and took to holding it like a viper in his own pudgy, wrinkled hand. "I'd think our primary concern at this time should be your wife, no?"

"She probably just went to the bathroom, yeah?"

It seemed the generals' opinions were not in accord when it came to this matter.

"She's not in one of the bathrooms! What do you think I was using the phone for? I'm trying to call her!" Ivle struck out in an attempt to reattach himself to his cellular. The attempt was unsuccessful. "—When this gets out, you're finished!"

"I'm retired." The general's lapels were just left-over ceremonial garb.

"Then what—? Then this is civilian theft!"

"Anything to take orders from a pretty lady," the general winked at Visen in confidence, but it was more buoyant than lecherous, and for that percentile distinction, she smiled back half a commanding press of her lips in a nod. "Alright," the evenness with which she surveyed the rest of the generals now regained any trust that might have slipped into second guessing her professionalism at the wink.

"In about five hours, on this phone," she held up her own phone, "I'll receive a call confirming our ability to acquire the paperwork that proves my claims. In the meantime, I want you," she handed her phone to another elderly general on her right, "to watch for texts from Nadia, Evelle's wife, and keep us updated. I'll just permanently disable the locking system," she had in fact opened the notes application on her phone and was now typing in, *'we have to delay the inaugural signing until tomorrow for my team to find the paperwork.'*

"Please show the screen to everyone else," she'd chosen the officer who'd seemed most embarrassed by the retired general's wink; if he was embarrassed, he had a greater chance of valuing Visen's authority; disapproving meant he might see her as pawning femininity to advance her own agenda. The officers passed her phone around.

"What is it?" Ivle reached—

"No—sir?" Visen redirected his attention away with one gesture forward, "let's go to the CCTV room, now; let's find your wife."

She half expected to find Nadia slouched in one of the armchairs of some unused room on their way upstairs to security.

But about 45 minutes into scanning live feed from every single CCTV guarding Swiverlia's state department, Visen's quick analyzing had turned into a quiet sort of dread. Nadia really was gone.

She wasn't in any of the hallways. She wasn't in any of the lounges.

More than once Visen'd jumped in relief at the sight of a seemingly familiar gown, but these, apparently, were the three or so like-minded potential friends at the gala whom Nadia had failed to find.

"Check the exterior. Check everyone who left. Do you have cameras at the side exits?"

"Of course,"

"Any news from Nadia?" Visen turned to her designated text-watcher, who had followed them upstairs. The Mertrian generals had arrayed themselves along the handrail of a platform that wrapped along the wall about three steps up from the security lab's main, tiled floor— presumably to keep an eye on Ivle, while continuously grumbling softly in discomposure.

"Nothing yet."

"Alright."

"Then go do something useful with yourselves!" Ivle exploded, "call the police!"

"Not using my phone though!" Visen didn't want it busy should Nadia call.

"I've got a few quarters," came a very old voice, "is there a pay phone around somewhere?"

"I've got a cellphone—"

"And get out! You're crowding; distracting!"

"Sir, you don't—" from the cold stare Ivle could just tell the old frog was about to pull rank.

"I am SMD of the Swiverlian Secret Police, now get the fuck out! And look for my wife!"

The little old frog had obviously been hurt but didn't want to admit it. "Doesn't really help your chances for interim presidency."

"Then get another plebiscite together and vote me out; you've got no proof of what this bitch says,"

Visen waved awkwardly from where she was overseeing CCTV read-outs. Visen was, evidently, 'this bitch.'

"Again, not the best at Public Rela—"

"Oh, Shut up!" Ivle lunged back into the chair beside Visen, whose own chair crowded next to the security guard in command of all CCTV monitors.

"There— right there—" Visen'd found a dark blur, exiting one of the building's side doors. It paused, hunched, over a cigarette. Not Nadia. "Damn. Can you fast-forward through any faster?" They'd already run through two side doors' footage for the night, but it took about five minutes for each door. There were 72 side doors.

"Look, Visen. I don't know what you think you're up to," Ivle side-eyed the Mertrian generals to clarify what he meant, "but you've been horribly misinformed!"

The Mertrian generals had subsided somewhat, back against the far wall, to allow additional security details to pass by, with updates on procedural measures undertaken the moment Ivle'd sent out a missing persons' alert. Ivle had to sign off on reports no other ambassadors had gone missing.

The procedure must've been part of the Swiverlian security allotted politicians' wives.

It was, apparently, quite common for Swiverlian politicians to raise the alarm so quickly at the slightest hint of an unaccounted-for persons associated with their political entourage.

He went back to whispering at Visen without taking his eyes off the paperwork.

"You've been listening to my wife for the past three weeks; you can't expect her to have a valid understanding of the politics at work here; now we need to talk about this before it gets out of hand—"

"—wait! Slow down a bit and go back—" Visen thought she'd seen—

Ivle glared at her. "What are you—?"

"Do you want me to help you find your wife or not?"

"Listen to me; Badmonkof was a cheat and a liar and he blackmailed all of us into doing his bidding,"

"Oh geez, must be tough; dunno anyone else who'd do that—" they continued scanning the live feeds.

"Why do you think I operate the way I do? Blackmailing potential career advancement isn't the same as threatening a loved ones' safety! But that's what Badmonkof—"

"I thought you were divorcing Nadia,"

"That doesn't mean I don't still care for her."

"She specifically asked if you'd hired me to kill her for you."

"Visen! That's because she's insane!"

"It's just—every time you talk about her it's like she's your own personal crucifixion in the form of an idiot; I don't think Badmonkof held your great love for her over your head, not when there were so many other black-mailable offenses—"

"Well why do you think I was the only one who had the freedom to act against him? Hm? I was the only one he hadn't managed to peg—"

"So, you *don't* care about Nadia, enough her safety could be used as leverage against you—?"

"No obviously I do! We're searching for her right now!"

"So she doesn't tell anyone what you've done."

"What have I done? Tried to make a nation run better?"

"No no no—that was always the point, wasn't it? That's why you wanted me to keep her from talking to anyone; you were afraid she'd run her mouth off—"

"Because she has no idea what she's talking about!"

"Then why not just come right out and say that?"

"I did!"

"No—I mean: are you afraid someone's gonna kidnap her to be able to use her as leverage against you? Or are you afraid someone's gonna talk to her, and figure out what you've been up to?"

"I absolutely fail to see the distinction,"

"Because—! Just because your wife's disappeared doesn't mean she's been kidnapped! Are we looking for someone whose primary purpose is to physically abduct your wife's body to use as a pawn against you, or are we looking for someone who mainly wants the ideas you're afraid your wife can convey to your detriment? It *matters* because if you're worried they'll use fears for her safety as leverage against you, they probably don't know you're going through an incredibly nasty divorce! That would narrow our suspects!"

"You really think you have any idea what's going on here? You really think you have any idea how a military government works?"

"Well if I don't please tell me so I have a better chance of doing my job!" They were silent a moment.

"I don't know what she sees in you."

Of course Ivle knew they were sleeping together.

"Now look, we've been tracking this position for months now," he meant the Mertrian presidency, "you're about to blow an entire strategic operation sky high; you understand me? You have no idea what's going on,"

"Swiverlia's positioning itself to take more direct control over Mertria; I know exactly what's going on,"

"And do you know why? Under Badmonkof's command there were thousands imprisoned and tortured—"

"You wrote up the list of their names for him,"

"What?!"

"Nadia told me."

"Are you an idiot?! Is this some sort of solidarity thing?! Just because you're both women doesn't mean you can trust a single thing that stupid bitch says!"

"Don't call your wife a stupid bitch!"

"Are you saying she's anything other than a stupid bitch?"

"Yes. Your wife is actually really cool; you just never spend any time with her! And now, you've gone and for all we know killed the one asset I actually envied you!"

"I didn't touch her!"

"But it'd be so easy, wouldn't it? Just write her name on a list and then you don't have to worry about her talking to anyone ever again."

"Oh geez— you know you girls've really gotta get it together, living up to this whole feminism thing a bit better than that, or the entire point of that philosophy's been misapplied; they shouldn't've let you run a military command; you're not thinking straight,"

"I don't see you having to prove you're qualified to anyone." They'd sped through the 76th side-camera by now. "There! Right there! Dammit, no. Alright, let's go round front and see if we can tackle that crowd around 9:30…."

They began counting faces that weren't Nadia's.

"You really have made a mess out of this whole thing, haven't you?" Visen couldn't help herself. She was fucked whatever she did now, unless they could secure the documents proving her claims. And then it wouldn't matter what she said to Ivle.

"You really think you're smarter than Nadia? Playing fast and loose with politics? You almost triggered a war pretending Livonians were smuggling weapons—" she'd been right about that; she could tell now by the smart snap in Ivle's eyes, "for what? So Badmonkof would listen to you? Badmonkof only listened to you 'cause he was sleeping with your wife, and if you think I find that any more of an intelligent way to lead a country you're wrong—but you snowballed everything out of proportion; you undermined every aspect of society that could've lead to peace, by thinking being covert in a self-satisfied way was the same thing as taking precautions for your own country's safety. And if it worked it only worked because everyone else was too stupid to take advantage of your inability to communicate— even Smutt only became a threat because you gave him the opportunity to— Wheeler told me: running round, playing God; you really thought you could outpace the randomness of time?"

They'd sped through the 76th camera overlooking the plaza outside the building's main entrance by now.

"That's exactly what politics tries to do!"

"Then play politics, not— personal vendettas."

"That's all politics is!"

"Then it's your duty to make it something else!"

Not a single dark shadow had exited the building, who hadn't subsequently reentered. And very few of them could've been mistaken for the silhouette of a gala gown.

"Try the back side of the building; any exits there?"

"No, it faces the sea,"

"Any CCTVs?"

"Three,"

Why so few? Oh —the monitors switched over— because it was literally just a blank cement wall running straight for three thousand meters under intense stadium lights.

"Dammit!" Nothing. "What about that dark patch to the right?"

"Runs down by the docks."

"Any cameras by the docks?"

"Mm… one by our trucking bay, yes," it was marked as frontal since it guarded such a large entryway; it was one of the cameras Ivle'd already swept through on his first visit to the CCTV operators.

"Well check again— What about that ship?"

"Hm?"

"That—private ship, no lights; out at sea; you can barely see it. How long has that been there?"

All night, apparently, though about 6:35, the camera recording it had been pivoted to one side. From then on, it filmed mostly the truck entry's side wall. "Is that unusual? For the camera—"

"No, not necessarily; it's an active bay."

What did that mean? They were bumping the cameras with their trucks?

"Well, what can we no longer see—?"

"Ah…. pivoted does obscure some of the walkway nearby. You could technically— yeah, you could sneak two or three people by there without getting caught."

"So, they could've taken Jacobsan too and that's why he's gone."

He was, after all, the lawyer to whom Nadia'd been feeding information.

Suppose Ivle'd been the one to get rid of them both?

He had a private yacht, didn't he?

"Alright; then let's say they went out that way—it's our best bet. Sir? Any text?" Visen had to bark her call back for the old general's hearing aids to register higher pitches.

"No." A backwards glance showed the general had been staring as intently at her screen as if it'd been a submarine radar. He was 86 years old. Good man.

Visen turned back to the screens. "See if anyone's boarded that ship," she pointed to where the private yacht could still just faintly be seen in the upper left hand corner of the tilted camera's livefeed.

"How can you even see that?" Ivle squinted at the mountain ranges that made up a black crumple against the computer monitor's sky; there was no ship he could see.

"Irregular geometry; always look out for man-made forms,"

"Why is it so dark though? There's usually a lighthouse—"

"They must've tipped the lighthouse off not to shine tonight,"

"You do hear yourself, don't you? In Swiverlia that would be illegal, and untolerated. This wouldn't be possible; it wouldn't be possible to kidnap the wife of a soon to be interim president because we have actual laws, that we follow,"

"I always got the impression you were against bureaucracy, holding all those unsanctioned meetings,"

"You trip this up Visen, you let the wrong men win,"

"The wrong men don't blow up hospitals. The —— hospital, October 1st. 3 years ago."

Ivle looked at her funny. "That was insurgents, remember? Insurgents who actually have a very valid point about the state of this country's infrastructure—"

"Infrastructure you built, and control,"

"For the betterment of people who would otherwise have nothing,"

"Right."

Oh God. He actually believed what he was doing was right, didn't he? He'd revolted as genuinely as the insurgents, and if he managed to get his way and unite Hungarian-Slavics into one Swiverlia, he'd have authorized all those proscription lists and exploded hospitals with impunity, because heroes always did get away with killing for their ideals. No one would even remember he'd murdered. Unless they could get Nadia to testify.

Chapter 41

Visen turned back to the security monitor. "Is there any way we can be absolutely sure no one's boarded that ship in the last 6 hours?" It was so dark; it was impossible to make out from visuals alone.

"Try sub-sonar." the text watcher raised his head, croakily.

Ah, selective hearing at its finest.

"Do you have sub-sonar installed? The Isometer team— just past the light house; it's Mertrian; you should be in contact." General Gavzen was very proud of having secured funding for those Isometer read outs, several years ago now.

"Uh, sir this is just an administration building; we don't have sub-sonar."

"Sub-sonar?" Ivle twitched. "It's a cruising yacht,"

"I'll call," one of the generals got out his own mobile and dialed the number of a friend who was head of the department for analyzing Isometer readings. Isometer readings, you see, could pick out the wobble of smaller boarding craft, plowing minutely submerged hulls through the water to meet cruising yachts.

Visen couldn't tell whether Ivle'd simply overlooked this fact or was purposefully going out of his way to stall them by being disagreeable.

"You already checked all interior and frontal footage, correct?"

"Yeah, just real fast, though."

The security guard handed Visen the mouse by which to control his monitoring station, so she could double check by zooming in on additional, random quadrants of the various screens. She began scrolling quickly back through all the banks of stored footage.

"She can't have just disappeared! It has to be that pivoted camera; it's our best bet; it's the only irregularity,"

"Maybe she slipped out among one of the crowds—"

"She was real noticeable—"

"Maybe she wasn't wearing the gown,"

"Where could she change?"

"Bathroom?"

"We already searched the bathrooms,"

In the back of the room, the general who'd called the Isometer team was just wrapping up his phone call. "Yup, yeah; ok! Thank you. Sir! —maim?" (he realized he didn't know which one Visen preferred to go by). "There's a pinging 500 kilometers south of here. Heading west. That'd put it near the beach, heading in the direction of the yacht."

"That's insane; a sub?" Ivle, again. He seemed genuine, this time.

"No, a little paddle board; must be too dark for the CCTV to pick out,"

In fact, the glisten of a gun against Nadia's neck, as she sat on the ocean-bound dinghy, with nothing but a slivered moon to illuminate its barrel, had been picked up by the CCTV footage; everyone'd simply mistaken it for yet another swell of gently lapping saltwater.

"So, you're saying someone rode out to that yacht on a paddle board?"

"Or something like it, you know, small— powered by hand," old generals oughtn't be expected to know the name of every new-fangled ski-do contraption.

"Alright then. Whatever it is, it's sketchy enough to check it out; can we zoom in on the boat's deck?" The security guard had to open a different program for processing the CCTV's image to help Visen out with that one. It still remained very, very blurry. "When'd the paddle boat go?" Visen called back to the Isometer-caller.

"9:36!"

"Alright; that'd be around the time Nadia disappeared; certainly didn't see her after that. Can you get the deck zoomed in anymore?"

"Ehh," a pixel about half a shade lighter around the middle of their screen may've been picking up on the reflection of a sliding door, but that was all they got.

"What are the Isometer readings on the yacht? Is it moving?"

Currently, the boat was backing away from the beach, slow enough so as not to make any noticeable ripples.

"Fuck." That didn't seem innocent. "S'cuse me. Sorry." She hadn't meant to reveal her own fears by swearing in front of higher-ups. "Alright; it's the only lead we've got; it seems promising; I'm going to go trace this; did anyone report to the police?"

"Yes, they're taking statements downstairs right now,"

Ah. *So that's where the general with the goatee must've gone.*

"Do you know of any soldiers under your command who came for the signatory ceremony?" Visen rejoined the generals crowded round the bannister at the back of the room. "Younger? Anyone who might be willing to help track that boat with me?"

If Ivle was up to something, Visen might as well just do her job and look out for double-crosses, the way she always did— whether or not she had the full picture, she knew she'd been tasked with finding Ivle's wife; if Ivle was the one behind Nadia's disappearance, so much the worse for him, thinking Visen would be unable to rumple his plans.

Alternatively, if Nadia'd left the gala with someone who was simply trying to interview her about her husband's underhanded dealings, Visen might want to elaborate on a few incriminating details herself.

One of the generals, a Hank Festze, knew a few officers at the gala who were young enough they might be able to help.

"No women I'm afraid; I've got one on signals, but she doesn't rank high enough to be here tonight, unfortunately—"

"Anyone'll do; that'll be fine; thank you," –actually, the discrepancy probably pointed to institutionalized inequalities in promotion. But the general'd obviously mentioned it in a misguided attempt to make Visen happy, assuming even now she'd have spare thoughts enough to wish for female companionship in the slog to diversify higher echelons—so now she actually was thinking about gender disparity; great!

And he was just trying to be nice! That actually made it worse somehow—a double pang of frustrated sadness for half a second— at the mismatch between motivation and reality— accompanied by a feeling of guilt for overriding appreciation of intent with sorrow at the fact he'd overlooked what his encouragement actually implied. To say nothing of being reminded about institutionalized inequality itself.

"Alright Ivle, we should have your wife back in no time. And, if she's not on the boat; we'll continue searching elsewhere,"

"I'll see if I can rustle up some of my men for a landing party…"

"Thank you, sir—"

"I've got to get to that signing ceremony—"

"No, it's okay sir; don't worry," one of the Mertrian generals played dumb, "we'll postpone till the morning— it's no big deal."

"No big—? We could crash the entire Mertrian stock market if we don't show foreign investors we're stable—"

"Tomorrow morning at 5 am— before the stock market opens—"

"No; I'm not going to put my personal affairs before my duties to the state—"

"Then consider yourself subpoenaed while we make sure you didn't do anything illegal to obtain this position—"

"What the—? There is no ability to subpoena interim presidents in this government!"

"There is in the Mertrian one."

Yes. And that sort of idiocy was precisely why they were now only semi-autonomous! Saying that out loud wasn't going to help Ivle, though.

"You can't seriously think any of those claims about my—whatever it may have been—Livonian-Mertrian struggles; you can't seriously think that's valid! I'm the one whose wife has just been kidnapped!"

"Well, we don't want to put her in any more danger; they might be using it as a ploy,"

Oh; trust the Mertrian military to confound a kidnapping investigation—!

"Holding off on assuming presidential powers is not gonna get my wife back! Not if whoever took her hasn't contacted us yet! It's 10:30!"

If they had kidnapped Nadia in order to call up and demand irregularities in the evening's proceedings, surely they would've done their research enough to know the signing ceremony was supposed to have been completed by 9:45.

"Sir we believe your wife may not even have been kidnapped," that general just seemed to straight up think Ivle'd killed her.

Ivle could only shrug at him expansively, shaking his head. "Ok? Then we'll deal with that once I'm in office; any police procedurals can be done with a sitting president; power vacuums, though, don't cut it!"

"Yeah, well, see that's just the thing we're not quite sure this newly revealed information doesn't bring into—"

"What newly revealed—?"

"The hospital—"

"The hospital's a non-issue!"

"We just can't be sure, if there has been Swiverlian interference—along with—civilian casualities," (they had, after all, been expecting some Swiverlian interference), "that this doesn't in any way go against our constitution,"

"It doesn't. There was an information packet. You were supposed to read. Before signing! Now let's go!"

The froggy little general who'd tried to pull rank didn't move out of Ivle's way.

"You're obstructing—. The overactive imagination of one woman, and you all go hysterical—"

"It's not hysteria; we've got proof of your involvement in at least five illegal operations so far."

"You have one person, who claims to have witnessed something they don't fully understand."

"No, we have three statements that corroborate one another." They'd managed to contact the lady whose party Visen'd slipped through, and one other regular schlub of a courier working for Ivle. "You're at least a blackmailer."

The little 86 year old General Gavzen had in fact been peering so intently at Visen's smart phone in an attempt to squint through reading a report Corvan'd just texted: the rest of Visen's old special ops team had already succeeded in tracking down 4 of the 5 blackmailed lackeys for Ivle she'd mentioned. Only Max, the IT man, was missing.

"That's a conspiracy to lie! Those are just statements. Easy to forge, easy to bribe—"

"It's enough to warrant a search party."

"Visen here gave you those names?"

Silence followed. Leveraging options, weighing atmosphere.

"You do know Visen has been using illegal amphetamines for the past two years, and that my secret services were the only men who caught her at it. I struck a deal with her; one of the first women SEALs; it's difficult; I understand; I tried to be merciful; I tried to give her a second chance. But the fact remains that she has a very good reason to want to get rid of me."

"Yes, sir she already told us that, to explain why she hadn't come forward earlier. Visen's in just as much trouble as you are."

Ivle and Visen eyed one another vindictively.

A black-buttoned policeman popped his head in the room. "Hey is there a Mr. Ivle in here?"

"…Yes?"

"We've had a report your wife's missing?"

Hah.

Ivle knew he needn't've tensed. They didn't have enough on him to send regular law enforcement out after him. Not yet.

"Yes, that's right; there've been threats against her before now,"

"We just need to ask you a few questions about whereabouts and ah when the last time you saw her was?"

Ivle realized he now had a choice to make. He could tell the officer Visen was planning to use military force against a civilian ship. But maybe letting Visen go do her thing searching for Nadia would simply get rid of her for the evening. He had an odd feeling the doddering Mertrian generals could be easily swayed by Swiverlian politique, once there weren't any disinterested parties in the room to witness how they could be coerced.

Then, he could simply arrest everyone on board whatever ship Nadia may or may not have boarded after he was made president, for conspiring against the safe turn-over of Mertria's executive powers….

He went with the police.

About four minutes later, Festze returned. "I've found a team of five for you; all amphibious landing squad except one, Jinkinze, who's agreed to keep an eye on visuals for you," —such as they were— "here in the CCTV room. He'll give you updates on the Isometer readings from here too,"

"Perfect; thank you." The team of five had trooped in after their superior officer's superior, thrilling at the pride of an opportunity to ensure he knew their names, and regrettably all still in parade uniform.

"We need to change clothes." Visen was still in her gala gown. "You don't have any tactical gear nearby do you?"

"Not any we'd reach in time,"

"Right." Of the six of them, Visen's gala gown really was the worst equipped.

She borrowed Jinkinze's outfit instead.

It fit in a pinch.

Jinkinze got a spare set of sweatpants out of the lost and found. The rest simply took off their jackets. "Alright. We'll need to commandeer some sort of craft; and weapons."

Of weapons, at least, the Swiverlian central administration had plenty. Lots of confiscated ones, due for processing.

"Oh my God; who smuggled a Claymore into this country?"

"Just take it,"

"It's too big to handle smoothly—" an odd model. "Does it come with a strap? See if there're any extra straps,"

A small, snub-nosed Heckler came with a strap; they quickly commandeered it. Visen described the flanking maneuvers she'd decided on as they walked towards the water—two of the men, Perkinze and Spitz, actually outranked her, but they'd all agreed to follow her lead, acting, of course, on their own initiative as the situation demanded. That was just the Mertrian military's way; a bit like herding cats.

Chapter 42

Two parking lots away, Gavzen's old rival, General Froybinitz, was doddering at commandeering a dinghy that had just driven by, attached to a truck he and a co-conspirator'd managed to force to pull over.

The driver seemed loathe to part with it.

"No. No you can't commandeer this dinghy. This is my dinghy."

"Special Agent for Swiverlian police," one of the Mertrians Visen had tipped off showed his badge.

If Ivle was working for Swiverlia, this was the first he'd ever heard of it.

(Ivle actually was working for Swiverlia— they wanted that Livonian and Mertrian land, dammit! Swiverlian bureaucracy was simply an absolute clusterfuck of parallel agencies all out of contact with one another.)

"We have authority to impound this property," Froybinitz took out a clipboard, "though we will properly compensate you, if you'll just fill out this form." But the look on his face as he handed over the paperwork seemed to suggest 'just you dare try claiming emotional damages.'

'Emotional Damages' was one of the little boxes civilians could check off to file reimbursement requests for contingencies. But it was usually only ever honored if owners had actually remained inside the commandeered vehicle at the time of subsequent operations.

Getting the dinghy down to the beach after acquisition actually proved more problematic. Froybinitz had found three dinghies to choose from, being near the water, but he and the Swiverlian agent had chosen this one in particular for the dark black polyvinyl chloride it was made out of—seemed useful for stealth tactics. Unfortunately, this made it show up glaringly ominous against the white-washed cement steps leading down from the flood-lit parking lot behind the state department to the beach.

Probably wouldn't have felt so noticeable if the dinghy hadn't kept flopping round on its trailer; Froybinitz could've sworn it was trying to scratch itself against every single cement surface it could find.

The rescuing party was already on the beach waiting for them, when they arrived, Visen receiving updates from Jinkinze over a headset they'd stolen from the gala's security guards, concerning how many meters out the cruiser had inched.

"Perfect; thank you sir." She snapped to attention when she saw the dinghy approach.

It kept flouncing unpredictable bounces over the wind, despite both generals' best attempts to keep it hip height.

"I think we should put a propeller in," General Froybinitz couldn't see how else to keep it from slapping against the water. It made for very poor disembarkation. He was used to much sturdier military installations.

"Propeller'll make waves."

"Alright—" Jinkinze crackled through the headset, "we're picking up signs of a second, smaller vehicle in the vicinity, about thirty meters west of the Anchorage lighthouse."

"That's us."

Right.

It was paddle-time.

They all crawled aboard awkwardly, then took turns feathering the water with their oars as sneakily as they could.

"Godspeed," the generals nodded from shore. Most. Ironic. Send off. Ever. They were headed out at about 8 meters a minute, making considerably less headway than the wind.

"Alright, you wanna steer West—to your right," this was Jinkinze trying to be helpful.

"Yes, thank you." They knew that— the waves weren't exactly helping things— they seemed to have a fervent desire to force the dinghy to steer left.

Alright, there we go; now they were full speed ahead. Wind had died down.

"Yacht's going at twenty knots now,"

Great!

That was about 19 knots too fast.

Jinkinze had transmitted in a local indigenous dialect, as per Mertrian protocol, in case the cruiser's radio happened to be tuned to the same frequency as Visen's headset.

"1000 meters out. They're slowing." Now the entire communiqué was in Reraytione.

"Standby." Why had Visen agreed to be 5th stroke? Coxswain should've been the one talking to Jinkinze.

"150 meters out. They're slowing. International waters in K minus 20 seconds at your current rate."

Now the fact it was so dark became an asset. At least the cruiser couldn't pick them up, unless it had some high-tech civilian echo-locater on board. But if it came from anywhere worried about political maneuverings in Livonia and Mertria, chances were, it didn't.

"100 meters." By prearranged agreement, regular communications now fell silent. Visen turned off the earpiece for now. Jinkinze would continue sending Isometer readings and unnecessary instructions through the stratosphere to throw off any eavesdroppers.

Now, there was no technology, nothing but Visen's team and the waves. She wished she had the thermal goggles with her. Moonlight glimmered faintly over the outer railings of the cruiser they targeted, but that was the only discernible movement on board, aside from the faint squeaking together of runners and amateur rigging, the awning's looped, metal overhang, like a wagon's top, teased gently by the wind, as the yacht slowed to a hault. They'd be in international waters by now.

The plan was to board the boat from all four sides; dinghy sloughing quietly round the cruiser's bow and out of sight after depositing Visen to the stern. She watched another teammate leap onto the boat's left flank; he gave a nod to Visen from where he hung on the railings, to signal a third had been dropped round the bow's starboard side. Visen nodded back, then twisted round to watch down the back side of the cruiser for their final boarder to dock. Their fifth, Sfeder, would remain on board the dinghy, for quick extraction and withdrawal. He caught hold of a lifeline Visen fed him off to one side. Now all he had to do was focus on not banging noticeably against the yacht's hull.

For a moment, again, there were only waves, the darkness, and the feel of wet metal railings grasped in each hand.

No one on deck. Visen made a sign for the man on bow, still in sight, to rise over the railings. His double, to the bow's starboard side, followed suit, to clear the forward cabins.

Five minutes later, the signaling bend of one man's arm round the boat's slicked, nouveau superstructure promised Visen they had skulked without incident.

She signaled for her own double to climb up on deck as she did, aiming gun and steely observation down each length of the boat's stern.

"Clear." He signaled.

"Clear." Visen crept forward to meet her fellow port side boarder, as per plan. The boat's superstructure on this side was lined almost exclusively with glass panels, opening into a single, enormous cabin. But only one of these sliding doors proved lit from within, by the faintest, dampened hue, made almost invisible by the tinting on each window.

Visen and her double from the bow, a marine named Perkinze, converged at the light. Pressed sideways, glancing backwards to see the room within, Visen could just make out Jacobsan, hunched at the side of a dining table build into the wall, about the equivalent of two state rooms away— it was a big boat. Perkinze saw him too, nodded, and tried the door. They'd been given pictures of the missing duo before they started out.

The door slid. Perkinze slunk in. Visen guarded outside, sneaking the door farther open to better enter as support if needed, though from what they'd seen, no one guarded the lawyer.

Jacobsan stayed motionless. He hadn't heard the door open. The yacht's inner chamber, down the side of which Perkinze now crept, extended what was essentially a posh cocktail bar down the length of the ship, draped in subtle greens and miniature fridges; it had enough leather seating for an in-home theatre, curving a leather couch, at its far end, round the circular table at which Perkinze could now see that Jacobsan had been writing. The dim, usually-reserved-for-romantic-dinners lighting by which he did so was what they'd seen through the glass door.

Perkinze nodded, for Visen's benefit, towards the lawyer's still-bent back, to signal he'd alert him to their presence. Visen shook her head. Perkinze shrugged: 'there's no one else in here,' Visen flattened her lips to bunch her cheeks to one side, nose wrinkled in a 'I kinda wouldn't in case of booby-traps?'

Perkinze went for it anyway.

"Jacobsan," he came to kneel softly by the lawyer, "Thank goodness you're—" but no sooner had his knee hit the floor, than Jacobsan pulled a gun on him and shot. Perkinze ducked to one side, grabbed the gun; but guards had already come rushing up from a secondary chamber below deck— a staircase which had no doubt once led to bedrooms in the bow. He was seized in a second.

"Ivle sent me—to make sure you hadn't been taken by force!"

"No, of course not; this is my boat. Tie him up, make sure he can't hear anything."

Shit! Visen doubled back from the open French window, lips, chin, and brow twisted into an ambient 'okey-dokey well fuck that than.' She didn't dare try to close the window; she could only assume if Jacobsan hadn't noticed when Perkinze first entered, the missing glass pane would go unnoticed, slid back as it was, unless it was moved again.

She stealthed her way up and over the bow's covered tip, keeping eyes on the cruiser's front windscreen, but no one was at the helm; they'd set the cruiser on autopilot, now they were drifting anyway. That was actually fairly advanced by Mertrian standards. Wasn't following coast-guard protocols, but if no one was manning the radio that could prove useful in a pinch.

She made contact with the two remaining on-boarders, Derkans and Spitz, signaling with her left hand, as she did so, by a slash to the throat that ended in an 'okay' sign and a hooked number 3, that Perkinze had been captured alive.

Three slices to the wrist with her left pinky meant 3 assailants so far accounted for in the room she had left. Then their signal for Jacobsan, and another slash to the wrist: Jacobsan, far from being another casualty, had apparently been the band's inside man on the job.

Spitz and Derkans reported back in the same, primitively efficient work-around for radio silence Mertrians had developed: no guards on the starboard side of the boat; again, one lighted cabin, visible halfway down the yacht's length, through a tinted glass door. Visen would bet anything that room was the same sitting room Perkinze had just entered—had to be open floor planning. They snuck back towards the faint glow this side of the boat to double-check.

In fact, the French doors on the boat's starboard side overlooked to a far greater degree the forward section into which Perkinze had been taken. Here the windows' tinting worked to their advantage; the lamp throwing reflections across their interior kept everyone inside from noticing three SEALs crouched just above them.

Visen checked from where she squatted: Sfeder and the dinghy could still be seen, trailing at an identical speed to the cruiser's almost stagnant shift along the waves, 25 meters back,

30 degrees to the left—a dead zone for any radar trackers—just in case the yacht did come equipped; they would pick up his dinghy as nothing but interference from what little wake the cruiser tried hard not to make.

Visen turned back to look down at where Perkinze had been brought to sit, bound— at Nadia's feet. Nadia was drinking a piña colada and playing Cube Bashers.

Chapter 43

"Did Visen send you?" she looked up when Perkinze was deposited.

"Who wants to know?"

"Oh, I'm not part of this; I dunno what's going on," she'd noticed Perkinze was attractive. She'd definitely noticed. But there was something disappointed about the way she redirected attention; she'd been hoping for somebody else.

"You two keep quiet. Did you come with anybody else?"

"Aah—" Perkinze had been distractedly eyeing where they'd placed his gun, just an arm's length out of reach, on the nearest counter, by a coffee maker.

"Did you come with anyone else?"

"No! I—they figured we could infiltrate easier with just one alone,"

"Well that was stupid,"

"Don't have to pay as much though, for the rescue." Jacobsan didn't look up from whatever he was writing. For a moment the muffled voices fell silent.

"I've been asked to negotiate with you," Perkinze bluffed suddenly. "I can get you on the same radio frequency as Ivle. He'll offer you a lot of money, if you give his wife back,"

"I don't care about his wife; we'll give her back once I'm done,"

"Done doing what?"

Jacobsan just gave him a look. Then kept writing.

"They want me to give a statement about what all's Ivle's been up to." Nadia disregarded all moratoriums on talking by pulling the gum she chewed out one side of her mouth, to play away anxiety, overcompensating with a show of laziness by examining her right hand's four inch nails, "Honestly it seems pretty above board; he's gotten into some super shady shit, honestly."

But why go so far out into international waters if they were just trying to record a statement? Mertrian, Livonian— even Swiverlian bugs only had a 250-meter transmitting distance, max. There was no reason to leave the shore so far behind, not in a cruiser this maneuverable. Unless— were they planning to meet someone? A rendezvous?

Visen turned her earpiece back on, to listen through the random yammerings of Jinkinze back at base. "Boat 2K7 78-99-4, 82-99-6—" those last were longitude and latitude. 2K7 meant 2.7 kilometers long. Big boat. Could've been a crawler; they came round the coast here, delivering produce and fish, mainly.

They'd boarded Jacobsan's yacht at approximately 78-99-3, 72-99-4. That meant the 2K7 was close, whatever it was.

Jinkinze reported a 996-gunner next, stationed two miles off to their left; but classification 9 meant it was Mertrian, not a concern. Unless Jacobsan was working for a Mertrian boss— but that would mean he and Visen were of the same persuasion, surely, fighting for Mertria's benefit, against Ivle.

Nadia opened the note taking application on her phone and typed, before tilting the screen sideways for Perkinze to read, but it was much too far away for Visen to see. She still grinned at the realization Nadia'd pulled the same stunt she herself had, trying to communicate with the Mertrian generals despite Ivle's presence.

Perkinze scanned the darkened windows round him, in hopes of making some contact with the rest of his team. The team crept silently round to a side window, dangerously open to the salty spray. Pop a head up too closely to that kitchenette's opening, and they'd be seen. Now if only they could find a way to be seen by Perkinze alone, so he could signal what Nadia wrote.

The top half of Visen's face popped into sight above a row of expensive vintage liqueurs. She glanced at Jacobsan. Still working. He was, in fact, designing the speech Nadia would read for a tape-recorder, once the details had been tweaked to match a reality she still hadn't fully explained. Jacobsan knew all the ways to make a testimonial airtight for Mertrian legal requirements.

The two guards who'd captured Perkinze went out to do a sweep of the ship; make sure he'd told the truth about coming alone.

Visen sent Derkans and Spitz to incapacitate them, buy some time. They rounded the bow's port-side at a crabbed side-sneak, just as Jacobsan's guards approached from starboard. Visen worked her way round the boat's stern. She could hear the squeaks of an unnaturally strained scuffing; silent hog-tying appeared to be underway. She rounded back to port side.

Here, an identical window to that over the kitchenette stood closed, but still in Perkinze's line of sight. Visen wiggled her eyebrows over a second row of expensive vintage liqueur, trying to signal Perkinze— then trying to stare into his soul to channel the sixth sense that would make him look up.

He was, at least, scanning the room for a means of escape.

Around his third scan he found his commander staring at him angrily over an alcohol cabinet. Oh. —Right.

She tilted her head towards Nadia's phone questioningly.

'Huh?' Perkinze didn't feel safe staring at any one spot for too long. His eyes swept back to Jacobsan, the gun, then back to Visen. She was signaling: 'phone. what. say.'

From Perkinze's face, it seemed they both realized simultaneously Mertrian signaling systems didn't work very well when your hands were tied behind your back.

Perkinze tried to mouth. It looked like a fish blowing kisses. "F. *F.*"

Visen seemed to have developed a twitch in her left eye.

No, wait, that was deliberate.

Morse! What was she trying to say? —'signal. using. Morse. like. this.'—oh right.

'S.' Perkinze started twitching.

Second letter: 'M.'
'U...'
'T.'
'T.'

Two 'T's? —Oh God dammit Visen might have guessed! Of course. Smutt'd been rifling through Badmonkof's paperwork when she and Nadia were—well, also rifling through Badmonkof's paperwork. Maybe they were both working for Mertria's benefit—?

'A...L...S...O'

Oh—yes? There was more?

'T... H... E...
'F
'R
'E
'N
'C
'H.'

The— wait. Like the entire nation?
'Come again?' Visen signaled. One of the guards re-entered to sit by Perkinze. Visen ducked. Then back up a bit. 'Come again?'
"The French," Perkinze tried mouthing. "F-r-a-nce."
"What?"
Visen ducked back down.
One of the guards had followed the line of sight that appeared to lead Perkinze into silently throat warbling at liqueurs. "Sorry— salt in my ears," Perkinze managed to smile apologetic, lame excuses just in time. He'd meant 'water'—in his ears—but close enough.

"Hey, y'know, whatever this French guy'll pay you—" he tried calling out again to Jacobsan, to get the focus of attention off himself. But it obviously wasn't loud enough to disturb minute concentration; he stopped awkwardly, mid-sentence.

"Jacobsan," Nadia got the lawyer's attention.

"Ivle'll pay you more than whatever this French guy is offering,"

"This French Guy?" Jacobsan's expression flatlined. 'This French guy' was vague enough Nadia'd obviously been trying to feed Perkinze information.

"Ivle'll pay more. Just get on the radio with him; I promise; I can get you on the radio with him; he's waiting for you; he's waiting for me to get in contact with him; he'll send more people out after me if he thinks there's been trouble,"

"You're a hostage negotiator?" Jacobsan tried to compensate himself for being very angry at having his speechwriting interrupted by taking pleasure in ironically hating how very much Perkinze seemed to misunderstand the situation he now found himself in.

"Yeah; you got a radio on this ship?"

Of course, they had a radio on the ship. Every ship had a radio— Blooming idiot.

Probably Livonian.

"No. We're keeping radio silence."

"Well they can't track you if you're out to sea; it's worth a shot."

"No."

But Nadia'd already put her phone to one ear, waiting through its tinny ringing. "He-yy,"

Expletives promised Ivle was on the other end.

"Your SWAT guy says you're willing to strike a deal with Jacobsan; you wanna talk to him?"

She reached the phone out towards Jacobsan.

"Nadia! —They'll track us!"

"They already tracked us!" she pointed at Perkinze.

"Yeah but now they can—"

"He's probably got a tracker on him; Ivle always does that; he tracked me once when I went to Switzerland," it had been justified. She'd claimed she was going to a spa. She was actually going to an underground gambling den. Not to gamble, just to watch, but Ivle'd still gotten completely the wrong idea.

She handed the phone over.

"Ivle?" Jacobsan wasn't prepared for this.

"Jacobsan. You took my wife?" Ivle'd gathered as much from Nadia's introduction.

"Yes. She's en route right now to tell Mertria all about what you've been pulling—"

"What the fuck Jacobsan! I wanna divorce her; she's not gonna tell you anything that's actually true; she's after fucking alimony!"

"Yeah. Sure she won't,"

Jacobsan hung up.

"Wait what about—the deal?" Perkinze winced.

"He's not gonna pay me money to keep her mouth shut," Jacobsan tossed the phone back to Nadia.

"—oop."

Nadia went back to playing Cube Bashers.

Perkinze began sweating slightly. What was going to happen to him?

Chapter 44

Out back, Spitz and Derkans were sweating too. They'd just spotted the looming, and quickly incoming, silhouette of Boat 2K7, gradually swallowing up what little sky the moon illuminated. "That's... not good." They'd already had to bind and gag two guards, then bribe them not to purposefully bang themselves loudly against the handrails. It wasn't like the incoming ship wouldn't eventually notice the two prone figures; there wasn't much out front to hide them under.

Spitz began spreading out a tarp inconspicuously to hide them, just as a third guard entered the control room to radio 2K7 in preparation for contact. Visen slunk round to where Spitz and Derkans had ducked out of sight, still subtly uncrinkling tarp, and signaled for Sfeder, with his dinghy, to stay well back, hidden in darkness; the 2K7's lights were newly LED; they only illuminated about 2 meters off the boat's side, but from their sheen Visen could read its serial number: Mertrian identification, white-washed on its prow.

As a 2K7, its Captain's deck would be on the ship's middle bridge, which spanned over the single cargo hold that made up its floating warehouse. Cargo crates were held fore and aft, creating three hallways, one down either side of the ship, and one perpendicular these, down the ship's middle, running directly under the captain's deck.

If whoever was—presumably—meeting Jacobsan on board (Smutt?) planned to question Nadia here in international waters, it was a good bet he'd question her in the captain's cabin. It would be the only place on board with electricity and privacy. If they took Nadia anyplace else onboard the 2K7, it was a good bet they'd take her to the crews' quarters—which were located in the stern.

Either way, if Jacobsan and Nadia did end up boarding the 2K7, Visen communicated in as small a whisper as she could, she, Spitz, and Derkans would board as well.

Derkans would take port stern, searching for Nadia there, if they lost sight of her; Spitz would take starboard stern. Visen bow.

If Jacobsan took Nadia directly to the captain's cabin on the bridge, same deal: Spitz and Derkans would slip over port side cargo, aft of the 2K7's central bridge, to which they now appeared to be docking, and make their way up the port-side hallway, along the side of which they could see coolies' rungs had been set in the whitewashed metal girders that ran the width of the cargo carrier. They could climb up these rungs, once Nadia's conveyers had passed by, to access the Captain's bridge.

If Nadia was stowed away, they should wait on top of the port-side cargo, to get a view of where, approximately, she'd been taken, then meet up with Visen by the stern.

No matter what, as much as possible, they had to keep visuals on Nadia. At any sign she was about to be shot, they'd open fire, aiming to kill but keeping one antagonist alive for questioning afterwards.

They didn't know enough about what this operation actually hoped to achieve to simply shut it down.

For as long as possible, they would hold back and listen in.

After all, they couldn't even really be sure Nadia was actually in any danger.

All this Visen communicated while constantly looking over one shoulder, to make sure Jacobsan's guards remained busy enough in the control room they'd fail to notice the miserable little team-huddle just outside their windshield.

The 2K7 had run completely parallel alongside Jacobsan's yacht by now, and Visen's small crew hunkered further down beside the yacht's railing, in an attempt to blend in with the tarplin.

From where they crouched, waiting, Visen could see Max, looking very un-IT like, help lasso a rope from Jacobsan's cruiser round a 6-inch-wide hitch on the carrier's stern. He still had his ankle socks on, despite the fact he now also carried a semi-automatic slung over one shoulder, and it struck Visen how very much she hoped they wouldn't have to shoot to kill. Max was just like her, pummeled into submission.

If this operation was running IT specialists as gunmen, though, that meant whatever was going on, it certainly wasn't professional. It was on the side, using people to whom leverage could be applied. But Ivle didn't appear to be taking any part in it, at least, not from the way he reacted to being called; they had Perkinze to thank for that.

At any rate, if IT carried Uzis, official Mertrian and Livonian government policy wasn't involved. Both countries may have been a mess, but they weren't that messy.

Visen, Derkans, and Spitz watched as Nadia walked out with Jacobsan to board the 2K7's plank way. An armed escort had come down to point guns at her back, but the whole thing felt so casual it might have simply been a defensive precaution. She kept on playing Cube Bashers.

As soon as she'd left, Jacobsan's remaining guards bound Perkinze down even tighter than before, and told him his night was going to be spent staring blankly at the cruiser's ceiling, waiting for them to come 'question' him after Nadia's interview. Honestly, Perkinze had no way to gauge how ominous that actually sounded. They were civilians; Visen's brief had included the fact Jacobsan knew Nadia from golfing together. Maybe this wasn't as bad as PTSD from past military exploits would have him believe.

The guards followed Jacobsan up the 2K7's plankway.

Visen re-detailed Derkans to go untie Perkinze as soon as the cruiser was cleared, incapacitating any guards they hadn't noticed who remained on board, un-hogtied. Once Perkinze could walk, they were to make their way up to the 2K7's captain's deck. If they didn't find Visen and Spitz there, they'd be able to overlook the entire ship until they could find them and meet back up.

But Visen's original hypothesis proved correct; it was, in fact, to the captain's cabin —nowhere else— that Nadia herself was now marched.

Amidst the shadows of the 2K7's overarching girders, the two silhouettes of Visen and Spitz, lithe and skimming, mirrored the general upward climb of Jacobsan, Nadia, and their posse, slinking round, then up rungs set in the deck's girders, to hide behind the metal siding of a cube-ish box mid-bridge that made up the Captain's cabin.

"After you," they could hear Jacobsan usher Nadia in first, to sit at the metal slab of a Captain's desk.

Smutt was sitting on the desk's other side, facing her; he'd been waiting for them.

Chapter 45

"So, you're French?"

The fact their interlocuter would be working for France was about the only elaboration Nadia'd managed to get out of Jacobsan.

"I work for the French, yes."

"Oh." Nadia sat, surveying the desk, which somehow seemed greasy, despite being made of steel.

"You mean like the country?"

"Yes…?" What'd she mean, 'like the country'? What other France was there? "I work as UN Police Task-Force Head, French Division."

"So, you don't work for Mertria?"

"No, I do. I just also work for France."

"How does that work?"

"Nadia?" Jacobsan decided to intervene, "don't worry about it; it's all perfectly above board, alright? I promise you."

"Yeah no no I was just trying to get it straight,"

"Alright," Jacobsan took a seat beside her. "So." They reviewed the documents he'd drawn up, Jacobsan peering over Nadia's shoulder as she annotated, elbow by the soon-to-be-used audio recorder. "So do you think it's phrased accurately?"

"Yah. Only I don't think he ever used the nuclear powerplant blueprints to blackmail Mertria, that wasn't part of his plan, at least not what he told Bravo 2."

"They were just—?"

"For Livonia to find,"

"I'd say that implies blackmail, yes?"

"Yeah, no it was more like he wanted Livonia to find them, so like, if you're going with blackmail, he wanted the blackmail-y bit to get out to the person who you'd traditionally be saying you'd keep the blackmail from as part of the blackmail, you know?"

"Ah, yep. Okay, yes, that makes sense," Jacobsan crossed out 'blackmail' and wrote in something about escalating hostilities instead.

"Now," Smutt subtly turned on the audio-recorder, "in order for this to be binding, legally, we need access to the documents that'll corroborate what you claim. Do you know where any potentially incriminating documents may be stored?"

Smutt knew that she did.

She'd told Jacobsan all about how Ivle was 'secreting office paperwork,' to see if it was nefarious enough to be grounds for divorce. And Jacobsan, though he may have reported how Colby'd been approached to turn traitor, certainly wasn't above turning traitor himself.

But something about Smutt spooked Nadia. She'd been fine with the whole plan when talking it over with Jacobsan, but now that they were sitting right across from one another— maybe it was something in the way Smutt smiled. Or the fact that he'd been after incriminating documents the moment Badmonkof died, same as her. Or, rather, the fact that he hadn't been trying to dispose of the lists that named inconvenient citizens for the state to exterminate, he'd simply been trying to change things around a bit, add a name or two, without anyone authorizing it. Or—at least, Nadia'd put very good money on betting no one had authorized him to go anywhere near those lists.

There was also the fact Galice had suggested so instantly Smutt was the one who'd killed her husband. Even if he hadn't, it still smacked too well of someone very clever going out of their way to never let anyone fully understand what they were up to.

"Uh, yeah…" Nadia paused as though analyzing how best to describe what she'd answer. "There's a little secret safe in Ivle's office,"

Did she really trust these men more than Ivle? She'd told herself it'd be okay, even if Jacobsan did have a gun. "It's just a precaution—to look official," he'd promised— but now she was beginning to think she ought to try to find a way to escape.

"That's the office that's not monitored by any CCTVs, right?"

"Yeah,"

How to get out of this without Jacobsan spotting she lied? She'd already told him everything.

"Can you be a bit more specific? About where the safe is?" Smutt leaned forward, as though itching to turn up the volume on the recorder, to make absolutely sure the mike caught this.

"It's in front of his desk," Nadia decided, "like, you know, the side of the desk you see when you walk in the study's door. From the hallway? Little button you press next to it."

Odd. Visen could have sworn Nadia told her and Wheeler the secret compartment and its button were on the desk's back, facing the side exit. She made a mental note to hope Nadia simply trusted Jacobsan more, having known him longer. But her heart tensed all the same. Why would Nadia lie? Did that mean this interview wasn't voluntary? Even if she had seemed relaxed on Jacobsan's yacht?

"So, the front." Jacobsan annotated. "Alright, and then we have the main access codes." Jacobsan, as Ivle's lawyer for Mertria, was also the one tasked with taking care of the Ivles' Mertrian summerhouse whenever Evelle and Nadia were away. He was responsible for facilitating the randomized weekly codes that helped keep Ivle out of court by sealing off his office.

"Of course, we'll need you, Nadia, to provide facial identification if we have to turn off the house's outer alarms," Smutt nodded.

"Right."

"And then how do we gain access to that wing of the house in particular? You claim here there's an additional code?" Smutt pointed to one of the notes Nadia'd scrawled as an overlooked aside as they reviewed Jacobsan's document.

"Oh?" Jacobsan hadn't noticed that. He hadn't known about an additional code either; he'd figured they'd just go in through the front entryway.

Nadia was hoping maybe routing them round back could help her escape, if she needed to. It was beginning to feel a bit like one of Ivle's summit meetings that usually ended with someone getting shot.

"Ah, yeah, it—bypasses a bit? The passcode's 2278." It was in fact 3725, and not entirely necessary unless one was determined to beeline towards Ivle's study using only the access route that led directly through cook's kitchen.

Nadia was hoping slightly false information might keep them in need of her. Of course, now she realized, if they didn't realize the information was faulty, it might not furnish them in time with any reason not to get rid of her, once she'd told them what they thought was everything she knew.

Shit. What if they didn't keep her round long enough to verify her claims? She'd been half planning to sneak away in the confusion of finding passcodes didn't quite match up—or something like that—she hadn't quite figured it out yet.

But she didn't want to look like she was purposefully withholding information. That'd make her look suspicious, right, if she looked like she was suspicious of them?

"Look I'm really nervous; can I have a drink or something?" She glanced between Smutt and Jacobsan.

"Ah. Yeah. Yavin!" Smutt called for a Livonian who was, evidently, actually captain of the ship. "Do you have any wine on board?"

"Yeah—coming right up,"

"No—no— I don't want that crap wine stuff that stuff makes me sleepy," she tried to laugh. "I want a cocktail; you had a cocktail bar back on your ship," she turned back to Jacobsan.

"Y-yes,"

Alarm bells reared urgency inside Visen's head: Derkans and Perkinze were still back there!

"No let's stay here; I don't think we need—"

"Look I wanna be comfortable if I'm gonna betray my husband, okay? This night has taken a huge emotional toll on me, like—emotionally—okay? Like I'm still scared you two aren't gonna keep up your side of the deal—"

"Nadia—"

"No I could just really use some compassion and comforting surroundings right now, okay? Like some actual alcohol,"

No, Nadia— please! if only there was a way to signal her not to go back to the yacht—

"We have whiskey?"

"I don't like whiskey," that was a lie.

"Nadia—"

"What? You promised me this wouldn't be involved; and then you go and tie up some guy—"

Smutt and Jacobsan exchanged a glance that promised Jacobsan would explain later.

"Nadia, please, this is very sensitive,"

"Yeah. And I want a fucking cocktail. You treat me like some kinda pawn I'm not gonna cooperate."

She breathed in a huge, shaky breath to calm herself down.

The men in the room side-eyed each other again for a moment. "Ok." They got to their feet.

This was the trigger Visen's muscles had been waiting for. She sprang, with a final signal to Spitz: 'fire as needed,' before flinging herself back down from the captain's deck to sprint the length of the cargo carrier's medial hallway in stealth mode, sneaking from shadow to shadow, light as a feather, bounding over the starboard-side hull to bump straight into—

"Derkans; Perkinze; quick—" she glanced back to see Jacobsan, Smutt, and Nadia were indeed heading back towards where they'd moored Jacobsan's cruiser.

"They're coming back to the yacht; Perkinze; we need to make it seem as though you're still tied up; we don't want them knowing there's more than one of us."

"You know how long it took me—?"

"Yes! Now tie him back up again; but make it as slack as possible without being noticeable—"

"I can't remember the specific knots,"

"They won't either—"

Perkinze pointed out where the rope had blistered into his skin at all its contact points. They could use that as an approximate guide for re-creating his initial position.

"Good man; thank you."

Derkans cut the rope, positioning its lesions behind Perkinze's back. They placed him within grabbing distance of his discarded firearm. Hopefully no one would notice he'd shifted position; he could've wiggled that far all tied up.

One of Jacobsan's guards now returned to prowl round the yacht's stern, preparing for re-embarkation. A 'bonk' and Visen replaced him as a seemingly still-subordinate slink of a silhouette for Jacobsan to see upon his return. The actual guard got hamstrung with his own shoelaces, gagged, and shoved under a bench on deck, where Visen could keep an eye on him.

Derkans crept away to hide round the front of the yacht's superstructure, just as Visen nodded deferentially to the returning Jacobsan, too shadowed for her face to be seen.

Jacobsan was followed by Nadia, Smutt, and Max—as gunman—along with 10 other additional guards— *(wonderful)* — and, finally—when he could be sure the 2K7's captain had gone back to worrying over paperwork—Spitz himself, bringing up the rear in a weird flanking movement that brought him flying down like a frogman just the other side of a metal railing round the stern's teak-and-chrome sun porch.

The ten extraneous guards filed into Jacobsan's interior lounge. Stroke of luck; they'd sensed a double cross and had now blacked out the interior's one exit with their massive, hulking forms. And of course, they were all facing inwards, because they were Mertrian mercenaries and they all wanted to be first to respond when Nadia decided to run for it. They could put it on their resume for future jobs. *'Foiled important espionage counter-moves.'*

"Why do you have so many guards?"

Visen could hear Nadia's faint drawl through the tactical gear of the ten men who'd failed to find her suspicious.

Actually, very useful question to know the answer to.

"Well, we'd originally meant to storm the gala, keep Ivle from signing the inaugural until we had the incriminating evidence we needed from you. We were all there, right ready to go—" *Oh, so that's why some of the mercenaries wore tuxes under their Kevlar....* "Luckily, you provided a perfect opportunity to just, take you aboard."

"We can always rescind the presidency later, with this," Smutt held up the recorder he'd brought along.

Sounded like they were doing precisely what Visen hoped to do, too.

"And of course, with you missing, the inaugural signing'll be delayed anyway; our men on the ground have already confirmed that."

"So, like, you would have kidnapped me?"

"Well, that was the original—"

"So that was *you* sneaking around my house two weeks ago!"

"Ah, no that was Jacobsan, actually. With my men."

"What the fuck!?"

At least that explained how the obviously incompetent frogman had gotten into Ivle's library that night. Jacobsan *was* the one who furnished all the access codes. But if he'd gotten in that time, how did he not know about the access code Nadia now seemed to be claiming they needed to enter the mansion's west wing? What was she up to?

"You were gonna kidnap me?!"

"No—I—" well, technically yes.

"Were you that weird freak in that webby costume thing in Ivle's library?" Nadia knew she'd recognized that walk.

"Uh, yeah I borrowed it from—" Jacobsan inched towards pointing out Smutt.

"Oh right 'cause French—so—you two have been infiltrating our government?"

"Ah, no." How did she—?

Well, France had been one of the Imperialist countries in the 1800s real intent on getting their hands on Mertria; no wonder they wanted to counter Ivle's posturing towards Swiverlian expansion.

"No, no we have a gentleman's agreement, to just make sure—"

"You killed Badmonkof!"

Again, "no—"

"No that really was an accident—"

"So, you admit you know how and why that trap was set—"

"Well, yeah, it was meant for you—"

"What?"

Visen had tried to tell everyone that!

"I knew you'd use that room to rendezvous with me on Monday; I thought it'd—snap you up when you came; I didn't realize that you'd—"

"What? That I'd walk through part of my house before Monday?"

"—*We shouldn't be telling her this—*" Smutt tried to signal.

"You said that part of the house was never used!"

"Except for rendezvous!"

"Well how many rendezvous do you have?"

"More than just waiting around for you to meet up with me on Mondays,"

"Ok, well that was a tactical error."

"That killed the—really? That was an accident?" They killed Badmonkof, by accident?

"An unfortunate accident, yes." Smutt had spent the last 4 years sidling into Badmonkof's good graces. The effort of so many unwanted golf tournaments, wasted.

"Why didn't you just talk to me?"

"That's what we're doing now,"

Jacobsan had actually had some idea Nadia might be more forthcoming and pliable if she was frightened—hence the, shoving her in a bag idea. Otherwise she might prattle, like she was doing now. He hadn't been wrong—!

"We just—needed to impress upon you that you need to tell the truth,"

"And you thought the best way to do that would be to kidnap me in a horrifyingly cartoonishly evil way?"

"It's not—cartoonishly evil—"

"What if Badmonkof hadn't come along? What if it'd been me? I'd've just been stuck in that bag for four days? I'd be dead!"

"Well I didn't realize— I mean obviously we had thermal sensors—" they hadn't actually realized they might need thermal sensors as a safety precaution. That house was so damn big; they'd figured—

"We're going through a divorce! Why on earth do you think you need *anything* special to get me to rat on my husband? I've already brought you all the information you need for the divorce anyway!"

Jacobsan hadn't foreseen Nadia wouldn't understand bringing down Ivle's good name would probably denude all the assets that'd make up her alimony.

"Well I couldn't be sure how—honest you'd be; I needed you to realize the international impact," Jacobsan looked to Smutt for help.

Spring-released bag in a hallway'd also been a much easier way to kidnap someone than storming a Presidential Gala!

Smutt was still trying to analyze whether Nadia understood she couldn't use the same lawyer as her husband to file for a divorce.

"I want a 'Sunset Boulevard.'" Nadia'd taken to sitting in a poutingly soulless jibe of a hunch where Jacobsan'd just been composing the confession she was supposed to be making.

"I don't—" lawyer looked at diplomat. Diplomat looked at lawyer.

Maybe this wasn't working out; maybe they should just go ahead and kill her.

"I'm not quite sure how to make that," Jacobsan finally realized 'Sunset Boulevard' must be a type of cocktail. "Can you make it yourself?"

"Yeah,"

Nadia was nervous. Her hands quaked as she undid the stopper for a bottle of Peach Schnapps she was pretty sure the recipe called for.

"Do you have cigarettes?" She got out a martini glass, set it on the bar between her and Smutt, and began pouring in little dollops of Southern Comfort next. Looked about right. Cook usually did this part.

She spilled a bit. "Fuckin'—" She tried to smooth it along the counter with one hand into inconsequence before anyone noticed. Then she spilled a bit more. Apparently asking for a towel was a bit too emotionally taxing at the moment.

"Um—cigarettes? Cigarettes?" Jacobsan looked up at Max, somehow both expectant and intimidating. Max had taken to guarding the room's sectional sofa; he couldn't seem to take his eyes off the man Jacobsan had tied up; Perkinze was now being guarded by one of the mercenaries, who'd strategically placed himself between Perkinze and Perkinze's firearm.

Smutt brought out a small cigarello from his breast pocket, with all the judgement of wondering how he could possibly be the only one capable of getting things done. "Will this do?"

"What is it?" Nadia picked at it with her nail claws.

"Cigarello,"

"It's not a cigar?"

"It's a small cigar."

"Why didn't you just say that then?"

"Do you want it?"

"Do you have a lighter?"

Smutt handed one over and Nadia lit up to one side with all the professionalism of a habitual smoker—intent first on testing whether the drink she'd made was palatable. It was not.

"Hey is this Southern Comfort gone off? Can alcohol do that?"

"Um, why don't you—I'll make you my own favorite,"

"Okay,"

"You just go ahead and sit down, yeah?"

"No, no I wanna watch you; I always like learning new drinks." She went back to focusing on why the cigarello wouldn't light.

"What is this? It's cheap—"

"You've got to—keep breathing in for a little longer, for the smoke—yeah."

"Oh. Yeah okay; it tastes nice— thanks," she pocketed the lighter, "what are you pouring?" she turned back to Jacobsan.

"Just a bit of rum—"

"I don't like rum."

"You'll like this,"

She did not like it.

Honestly Nadia? What the fuck.

"Ok I'll—make you another piña colada alright? Just go ahead and sit down with Smutt. Let's, try to get this show on the road, yeah?"

It was almost light out by now. The dinghy had dropped back; Sfeder sorely missing being covered by darkness. 'No. No no,' Visen signaled by slashing one hand across her throat from the yacht's prow. 'Come forward.'

She was the only one guarding outside now— safer for the 2K7 to think the dinghy came attached to the yacht. They'd have to play musical chairs with it, moving round the boat's circumference in an attempt to always keep a diameter between dinghy and enemy. But if anyone onboard the 2K7 thought it looked suspicious, there was, luckily, no one in the radio room currently to hear if they tried to alert Jacobsan to a bogey off his bow.

Spitz and Derkans remained immobile, trying simultaneously to keep hidden and look through the yacht's side windows.

Nadia was still slouched beside her failed cocktail, sipping her new one scientifically. "No, I don't think I like this it doesn't go well with the cigarette," she noticed a smudge of something on the bar top and tried discretely dabbing it away by hitching up her gown and patting. Now the side of her ball gown had Southern Comfort all over it. "I think I'm having a panic attack; can cigarillos make you lightheaded?"

"Jacobsan?" Smutt had been scanning the news on his phone while waiting for Jacobsan to finish pampering his prima donna.

"—Try maybe to sit down, put your feet up," –they could conduct the interview that way—

"—I'll take my shoes off—"

"Jacobsan!"

"Yeah?" He finally had a moment to come to Smutt's side. "What is it?"

"We're fucked. Look at this:"

The Mertrian Post had woken the world that morning with an exclusive interview detailing the worries Visen had passed on to Mertrian officers; one of the generals had apparently told the police all about her suspicions—and of course police procedurals were precisely the sort of watersheds to which reporters always found it criminally easy to listen in. They even mentioned rumors about a secret compartment in Ivle's study that hid incriminating evidence.

"A search and desist warrant is expected to take effect this Thursday, at which time reports can be confirmed."

"It leaked."

"So Ivle's compromised now anyway,"

"Fuck,"

There went a controllable interim president.

"Who could've possibly—?" they both glared over at Nadia. "Have you told anyone else about this?"

"About what?"

"The—crimes you believe Ivle may've committed?"

Well, there'd been that lady at the funeral; she'd told Wheeler a bit—but mainly, "my bodyguard, I guess. but that was just so she'd make sure not to let you guys kidnap me. She didn't tell anybody; she didn't believe me. Look do you have a hot hand towel?"

"A hand towel—?" was she drunk or just horribly inexperienced when it came to basic human politeness?

"For my—" she gestured at her head.

"Sure." Jacobsan rattled off to go collect one from the bathroom, running water.

"No not wet; hot!" Nadia turned back to find Smutt had his gun pointed at her. He didn't even bother explaining why they no longer needed her, he just fired.

Chapter 46

Oh my God no time for hot cloth; Nadia had enough of what she needed— she pinched Smutt's lighter open almost on instinct as she ducked down round the bar, forcing the hand that held the lighter to stay atop the bar's linoleum—despite what gunshots may come—to spark off the pool of alcohol she'd spread out— a flash of flame flared across the bar, hissing pops to leap up, keeping her hidden, blocking Smutt's gun with its flush of a blooming roar.

"Active shooter!" Visen's team leapt in, or, in Perkinze's case, out of his faux knots; the bar's flames flaring up at almost the same instant as the windows above and behind Smutt shattered.

Nadia stripped off her dress, grabbed a bottle of Tequila she'd left uncorked and shoved the already flammable gala gown through its spout, rushing the flame from Smutt's lighter back and forth across its surface only to realize she didn't have time— Smutt was round the bar, gun raised; he'd dived the instant Spitz and Visen crashed in towards him; his gun was up; the Tequila lit; Nadia threw the whole thing, gown, bottle, and flame at Smutt— Molotov one away! Her new favorite kind of cocktail.

It was lucky she'd thought to pre-swab so much of her dress with that Sunset Boulevard spill; the fire had spread instantly over its fabric, covering Smutt's head for a bewildering, screeching second in flame before he managed to tear the melting polyester off in one primal swatting sacrifice of the hand his amygdala deemed less important than his head; the polyester stuck to his palm; it stuck to his forehead, ear, and cheek where it'd hit; he rolled and screeched doubling over and banging against the bar's end as though blunt force trauma could fan out the flames.

Visen had him face to the floor in a second, arms whipped round into cuffs so fast they probably broke, having rushed to knee him in the back from the adrenaline of smashing Max unconscious as she shoved past in one motion.

But Smutt cuffed and—for the most part—deflamed, meant she still had to fight off the 10 mercenaries, who weren't taking cribbed shots. Derkans had laid down covering fire to scatter Jacobsan's security as Spitz and Visen dived. Now, he came down through the windows overlooking the stairs that lead down below prow, as Spitz took over covering fire, knocking Jacobsan out with one backhand, that then knocked the lawyer out a second time by sending him flying into the space-efficient bathroom sink just behind him.

Perkinze had bonked his guard with a swift, unexpected cuff to the ear and regained his weapon, using the guard as human shield to shove against the would-be fatal fire from what were now nine silent, buff, well-coordinated mercenaries very happily shooting semi-automatics from behind the cover of a steel-integrated leather sofa.

Two had instantly aimed their guns at Visen's back, but they couldn't shoot or she'd shoot Smutt. Perkinze shot one; Visen spun round to take the other's gun as he pivoted to aim for Perkinze, knocking Smutt out with the same backward crunch of a heel that plowed her into Perkinze's would-be shooter.

Two mercenaries ran outside to check their rear, caught sight of the dinghy, and instantly started firing. The dinghy popped. Sfeder slipped under its wreckage. One stayed, waiting to see if he'd resurface.

A third shot at Spitz; he was hit. Visen shot the man who shot Spitz, with the gun from her would be guard, just as another mercenary leapt over the bar's fire to catch Nadia. The fire had spread, soaking along the leather interior with a foul, plastic smell until it hit the kitchenette cabinets with an explosion; apparently, they'd been storing ammunition under there. That took care of the guard who'd gone after Nadia, just as Derkans joined with a guard who'd beelined to take out the wounded Spitz. The guard managed to take out Derkans instead—

Another pair caught Visen, two guns on either side of her head this time, just as she managed to rush past Smutt to peer over the bar's barrier of dancing flames and see Nadia had disappeared.

Phew.

Also, what the fuck? Where was she?

"Who are you?"

Thick Swiverlian accent.

"Nadia Ivle's bodyguard."

One of the guards from outside had returned to execute Spitz and Derkans. Perkinze was playing dead unconvincingly.

"Look, don't shoot my men and I'll help you find her. I'm a mercenary. My first priority is to keep my team safe. We'll give you no more trouble. You won. We lost our salaries. It seems like she's probably already dead anyways."

"She's not back here,"

One of the guards had gone to apply first aid in the form of large white towels to the skull of the man who'd been depth-charged accidentally by the kitchen cabinets. He'd managed to drag himself away from the flames.

"What we need—"

"Don't move!"

She'd only wanted to mention they could use a fire exstinguisher.

Well, if they wanted to drown awkwardly amid flames….

On second thought, Visen knew enough about boats to realize hiding in one of the efficiently secreted away storage units for things like extinguishers would be right up Nadia's ally. If she was still here and they searched—

"Check under the seats for a fire extinguisher!" Someone else gave the order.

A clattering and banging commenced, flames still lapping ominously, as black clad guards ransacked the ship's interior, while Derkans crawled over to Spitz in an attempt to stop his bleeding. Visen didn't need to signal: 'tourniquet'—though she tried—he was already on it.

"You sign Mertrian?" the guns on either side of Visen's head slacked off about an inch from both ears.

"I am Mertrian," Nobody bothered learning Mertrian sign language except Mertrians.

"You were sent by Ivle to keep his wife from testifying?"

"No. I'm just supposed to keep her alive. I was fine with everything until he tried to shoot her," she nodded down at Smutt, whose first aid was a bit more rigorously official with its various oozes and bandages from a medic bag strapped round one of the guards. He was just coming round.

The sound of foam spraying downstairs meant the fire extinguishers had been found. And also that this boat was probably unstable by now, if flames had reached wiring that close to the prow. —Where was Nadia?

"Did you know your boss is positioning himself to take over your country?"

"Yes; I just heard—" she gestured to indicate she'd heard when Smutt read it out loud. Visen wasn't quite sure how they'd react to knowing she may've been the one responsible for leaking that news to the press.

Of course, how the hell *did* all Ivle's well laid plans have anything to do with the Mertrian presidency, if Jacobsan admitted Badmonkof's death had been an accident? Unless each counterstrike in this stupid game of cat and mouse facilitated opportunity the counterstruck could seize, ensuring all one another's worries were self-fulfilling prophecies.

The mercenaries raised their guns again. "Nadia told us she told her bodyguard about Ivle's plans earlier."

"She did. But I didn't connect it to the fact it might have anything to do with angling for the Mertrian presidency until Smutt started reading that article out loud."

"And yet you are still loyal to Ivle?"

"No, I just told you we're mercenaries; we don't care about this; it's just our job."

"So, you did know the man you work for was purposefully undermining your government?"

"No, obviously not or I wouldn't't've taken the job! I thought it was just to keep Nadia safe. If what you say about Ivle is true, I am no longer on his side I'm on your side, but you have to tell me what's going on," her eyes kept flicking round the half-obliterated cabin. No Nadia in the rear corner. No Nadia by the TV.

"How about you tell us first where Ivle's wife coulda gone?"

"Why don't you tell me why Smutt here tried to kill her?"

Both guards and Visen eyed Smutt, who was peering beadily up at them through newly applied dressings.

"I… honestly don't know; we're just security."

"Right."

No Nadia by the shattered French doors….

Just a huge, gaping hole where a window had been, right behind the bar.

Had she jumped out? The window had been open long before the fire—that was right. It was the window through which Visen's team had initially peered in an attempt to contact Perkinze. It was small, but Nadia did gymnastics. And she had promised to leave if emergencies arose, that'd been part of her tactical evasion training…. Hopefully, with all the scarred wreckage round that side of the yacht now, Smutt's men wouldn't notice the window could have provided her with a means of escape.

"He's coming round—" Visen pointed at Jacobsan, eliciting nothing but an irritated groan from Smutt, who had just gotten to his feet, still hobbled by Visen's handcuffs. "You okay?" he came to stand over Jacobsan.

"Yeah," the lawyer blinked from where Smutt stood handcuffed to where Visen stood under gunpoint.

"Then help search the ship. Nadia's gone. Search the ship!" Smutt called out louder to the guards filtering through from downstairs, "she has to be here somewhere!" he paced towards the nearest scorched wreckage to kick at it with all the savageness of a preoccupied mind.

The remaining guards who weren't medics, injured, or pointing guns at Visen clumped off to join in the search. Perkinze tried to stop playing dead but was instantly cornered by a rifle.

"You need our help more than you'll admit." Visen addressed Smutt now. "You think this was sanctioned by my superiors? You think I want to lose Nadia?! You don't kill her, you have a professional SEAL team at your disposal!"

"Ok. Then we won't kill her. Where do you think she went?"

"Why did you try to kill her once Mertria found out about Ivle?"

Visen had her hands up and two guns pointed at her. But that didn't mean she couldn't still carry out her own investigation.

"No talking."

Aaaand now the guns were back to sticking straight against her head.

"Where is she?"

"I'd check the closets."

Might, hopefully, give Nadia some more time to swim away from the boat, if Visen's hunch was correct.

Didn't trust Smutt worth a shit.

"The closets?"

"Yeah all the closets; it's where she hid from Jacobsan last time."

The cruiser's designers had made excellent use of negative space by covering the boat all over, where possible, with lightly polished cherry wood and calling it 'built in wardrobes.' There were about twelve of these little nooks, not counting the less obtrusive ones small enough the probability they'd be overlooked might actually make Nadia consider hiding in one of them. At the very least, rifling through all the coat hangers might delay searchers long enough Nadia could slip away. She would remember to make a run for it, wouldn't she?

"See, if you explain what's going on, I might be on your side," Visen kept bluffing, half serious, "I might be able to make that recording you wanted from Nadia; she's told me quite a bit, and I've been in Ivle's pay for 3 years now. If I understand what your angle is, I can help—"

"You just don't want to be shot do you?"

"No; I don't."

Why was he acting like that was a weakness?

"Alright." Smutt could always shoot her afterwards. They were in international waters. No one checked shit out here. "I work with the Gendarme de l'Unité Internationale; UN Police Task Force, French division."

Right. Visen decided it'd be better to pretend this was news to her.

"We've been watching the situation in Mertria and Livonia for quite some time now; your countries need help. So, Ivle works for us, otherwise, we tell the world what he's done to inherit the Mertrian presidency,"

"So, he did kill—"

"No, the—"

"Playing off, the—semi-autonomous—against each other?"

"Yeah."

"So… you're blackmailing him?" How many layers did this blackmailing policy have anyway? It was like a Pyramid Scheme.

"Mmm," 'blackmail' was such a nasty word. "This was just going to help open up negotiations. Of course, if Mertrians already know he manipulated the situation with Livonia to his own benefit, we have no leverage. In which case, it'd be best if no one found out about this," Smutt revolved a forefinger to indicate the entire boat-bound enterprise.

"You can make sure of that without shooting anyone; I don't want news of this to get leaked either—it looks bad for all of us; I'm sure it wouldn't help Nadia with her divorce; she doesn't benefit by telling people she gave away all her husband's secrets; isn't there some sort of anti-alimony clause about that?" That'd make sense. Cultural memory was prompting Visen to recall some neighbor's tiff about giving away a husbands' company's secret formula. "She wouldn't exactly want news of this meeting leaked either,"

"Right. So, as you say, we don't shoot her."

Visen wondered idly if Max was here because Smutt and Jacobsan had leveraged the same blackmail against him as Ivle had. Seemed they weren't much better than OPSAI, but potentially more useful for maintaining Mertrian autonomy....

"Look how much information about Ivle did that article give out? Because I have several examples you can use of how he played Mertria and Livonia against one another; I'm sure they can't have gotten everything." For example, Visen was still having difficulty believing Badmonkof's death had been an accident. They could probably pin that on Ivle.

"We think—"

One of the guards started shooting into the water—

"Stop! What are you—!" Visen lunged forward, worried for Sfeder, but her two guards' gun barrels pulled her back by the temples— "Ow—"

"Shine the light—! Thirty knots to the left!" one of Smutt's subordinates had picked up Jacobsan's intercom and was radioing the nearest lighthouse. They had, apparently, bribed a whole string of lighthouses along the Mertrian-Swiverlian coast to do their bidding, because, almost instantly, a giant, sweeping light whisked on, blindingly flared in the early morning twilight.

"There—there!"

It illuminated the small, swimming form of a very naked Nadia, paddling along.

"Where is she—? What the—? Dammit! Shoot! Shoot at it!" Smutt careened into his subordinate and took the transmitter away. "Keep your light on the girl!"

"What are you doing?! You still need her to confess!"

"No, not necessary. We have you now."

"You're not the fucking UN, are you? Cut it out!" Visen grabbed both guns guarding her at once, and brought them jerking forward over her shoulders into one another until she could pivot them over to smash down on Smutt's head, whipping around, when he crumpled, to maim her left-hand guard in the solar plexus, the man to her right in the forehead— before spinning round to aim one rifle directly at the kidneys of the man who'd taken to firing on Nadia. "Drop the gun!" She miscalculated how far he was from her and jutted the rifle's barrel squarely into his side—made him drop the gun faster. "Nobody move!" she dragged him round to sandwich herself between his body and the handrail, forcing him to kneel, and bending over him, gun to his head. She quickly repositioned from death grip against his jugular to holding the gun in a way she could actually shoot it. Her other guard's gun remained stashed under her left arm, digging into her side. They were in sight of the shoreline by now.

"Put your hands up all of you!" About eight of her enemies weren't incapacitated, compared to her, Derkans, and Perkinze— and potentially Sfeder, if he could come up. That'd be two to one—

She noticed Jacobsan, who'd crawled outside despite his concussion, put his hands up too.

"He lied!" she frowned a quick nod at Smutt's crumped form. "Tell me why you shoot at Ivle's wife! Now!"

Her gun jostled into Nadia's would-be shooter's temple, but the command was really directed at anyone who wanted to save his life.

"Now or he dies!"

Silence.

Ok. He died.

"You're next!" Visen pivoted to bring her sites dead center, on the guard just now recovering from being whopped in the solar plexus.

"The idea's—Stop! Don't shoot!" Jacobsan cracked. "The idea's that we don't want anyone else getting the information or we have no leverage over Ivle,"

"That's what he just said," she meant Smutt. "Try again!"

"If Ivle's in command, we need to be the only ones who have control over that information!"

"Nadia won't talk!"

"No—! We need to have sole control; even if there's been a bit leaked, we still have a chance—as long as Nadia doesn't tell anyone; that was always the plan—"

"Don't you go golfing with her sometimes?"

"Yes?" Jacobsan failed to understand the question. Visen failed to understand how he could sacrifice his friend so easily.

"So, you were just— gonna kill—"

"You just killed!"

"Because the surety I'll shoot's the only reason I command this ship. Why do you need that kind of control over Ivle? If you act solely to stabilize Mertria, Nadia doesn't benefit from telling anyone she sold out her husband to you. She'd only ever pose a threat if whatever you plan would somehow be worse for her than losing all her alimony to some 'mustn't give away husbands' secrets' contingency. So, what would make her talk? Why do you need to be the only ones who have/to have this level of control over Ivle? So you can force him to sell Mertria to France? No matter how much that countermands Swiverlian policy?"

That'd tank Mertrian finances, with even more disastrous results for people like Nadia than a failed bid for alimony.

Oh ho ho. Some of the Swiverlian guards had pricked up at that, beginning to realize they may have been operating under the same sort of contradictory interests they'd just accused Visen of betraying her country to.

(Of course, they all knew Swiverlia hoped to expand into fully controlling Mertria. That was so obvious it'd always been a non-issue.)

"Ab—what? No! We're— France wants to help—the UN—Mertria needs reform! That's what we're—"

"Keep telling yourself that," Visen grinned, play-acting insight in hopes she could convince him she'd enough he'd feel forced to keep talking. "You've already lost out to whoever reported to the Mertrians anyway!"

"Not necessarily!"

The man under Visen's gun gave Jacobsan a 'really? She's gonna fucking kill me!' look.

"What do you mean?" Visen flexed her gun, angling preparatory to firing surer.

"Um. Well. I mean, you said you had more information than Nadia did; I'm sure we can strike a deal—" Jacobsan was getting flustered now.

Visen began to wonder if the concussion was actually working to her benefit. Had he just betrayed some—

A splash came from out back. Someone had dived after Nadia. Someone unaccounted for.

"Line up against the handrail; all of you; hands on your heads; kneel! Now!"

Up until this point, a little further past the burnt superstructure's shell than the rest of the men out on deck, one of the mercenaries had been holding his gun to Perkinze's head in a frozen daze, not quite sure if Visen had seen him yet.

He watched now as the rest of his team knelt, so she could scan out to sea in search of whoever'd jumped overboard. They all seemed to have calculated (correctly) that none of them were in a position to draw fast enough to shoot Visen before she could mow down the lot of them.

Now she noticed Perkinze's predicament.

"It seems I have you at a slight advantage!" she called out. "You kill one of my men I kill three of yours. You don't get over here right now; I kill three of yours anyway."

He'd seen her shoot the last guy. Perkinze's guard dropped his gun and went to kneel with his mates.

"Cover them." She gave her gun to Perkinze. "Keep eyes on Nadia at all times." Nadia was still swimming.

Visen ran back through the cabin. Max was still sprawled but coming round. Derkans had stabilized Spitz. "How far are we from land?" he whispered.

"About 1/2 a mile; use the captain's intercom; ask for bearings; Perkinze is guarding the men; Spitz; you doing alright?"

"I'll be okay,"

"Alright. What jumped off the boat?"

"Guard at the back,"

"Why—?" She ducked out back. How many spare guards were there sneaking around?

She scanned the shoreline to find—Nadia's house.

"What the—?"

Chapter 47

Sfeder had remained floating in his disguise as waterlogged dinghy scraps, unaware of on-cruiser victory. Visen now noticed the crinkled mini tipi in the dinghy's side he'd been using as an eye hole.

"Sfeder! Get out of there!"

The eye hole hadn't been working that well; at the moment he could only see the boat's hull, and he hadn't wanted to be too obvious about repositioning.

"Visen?"

"Get outta—there—!" He came up blinking sea salt. "How the fuck'd we get back to Ivle's?"

"Going 22 knots an hour; 2 hours approximately; it tallies." Glad to know he could still keep track of that kind of thing underwater.

Jesus; they shoulda just gone by boat to the inauguration. That would've been so much faster. Also, probably not moving in accordance with water vehicle regulations, but still!

Of course, if Jacobsan and Smutt had charted a course to meet near Ivle's house… even accounting for the slippage in location that came from struggling with surprise mercenaries amid conflagration… they were planning to go after the incriminating documents in Ivle's study, soon as Nadia admitted their precise location as part of their 'testimony.'

They wouldn't wait for Interpol, or whatever the UN called peacekeeping nowadays. (Visen wasn't up on UN lingo, being from one of the few countries the UN still considered "3rd World").

No, Smutt'd take the documents for his own benefit; Visen's testimony against Ivle would never be proven; and France'd be able to pressure Ivle into subordinating Mertria to their Commonwealth, just as Smutt planned.

That'd happened to Soothsan just last year.

And at least one member of Smutt's team must have been briefed on the plan, because that'd explain why he'd known to jump overboard upon arriving at Nadia's house; en route to using the passcode Nadia's interview had provided, he could drown Nadia herself for being an irritant of a loose end. Visen could still see her paddling, mid-bay.

"Ok, Sfeder, come on— come up—" she helped him on board. "Spitz is down; Perkinze is guarding their remainder; Derkans is at the wheel—"

Oh shit Max was sitting up now.

"You!"

As good as any.

"Tell me why we're at Ivle's house now; why did we chart a course to Ivle's house? Answer me!" she punched him.

Now he had two nosebleeds. "They're gonna go in and take the files in his office to blackmail him,"

"Awesome." Two-pronged approach then, Nadia and the files; Visen'd been right. "Thank you; just checking. Derkans call in a burglary in progress at the Ivle's mansion at 66 Cleveland!"

"Mayday—Mayday—"

"Use the phone," she shoved one into his hand. "Sfeder come with me; Derkans guard Max—"

"Max?"

She pointed.

Derkans repositioned his gun, still on the phone. "Yes? Hello? I'd like to report a break in—"

"Sfeder—you've been shot."

"O-oh." So that's why they'd been so convinced when he played dead; must've been billowing blood out from under the dinghy. He was also apparently suffering from early onset hypothermia.

"Here. Get in the shower," Visen ran cold water over him, dashing off to steal a medic's bag from one of the crouching guards, and shouting "good work Perkinze," without looking back over her shoulder as she dashed back, all in a manner of seconds.

"Derkans, fix Sfeder's leg; Spitz? Still stabilized?"

Spitz nodded.

Derkans signaled he did not in fact have a third hand with which to help Sfeder at this time.

"Just—figure something out; speaker phone." she punched the right button for him, then dashed back out to the cruiser's side railing, to watch as the lone escaped guard made contact with 5 shadowy figures on the beach head below Nadia's house. He'd swum round to a prow of jutting rock on the bay's far right-hand side. Nadia was still struggling placidly through the bay's center.

Visen's phone rang.

"Hello?"

It was Corvan. "We've got a warrant to search Ivle's house, so you can expect a task force within one to two days—"

"Ah fuck." Visen just hung up on him.

Then texted 'thank you' without looking down at her phone, to let him know she hadn't died.

Hopefully the local constabulary would be quicker responding to a robbery. She'd bet good money those figures on the beach were trained to kill on sight....

But that phone call'd been enough; now she couldn't see—

"Perkinze!" She rushed back up to him then slowed instantly into a whisper so their prisoners couldn't hear (always good to keep 'em guessing as much as possible, in case one escaped later). "Where's Nadia?"

"Just made landfall." He pointed. "I'd say she's about a quarter mile up the beach from the mansion on the hill,"

"Thank you."

Nadia'd be trying to get home again, then.

Even swimming for her life, too far below the cliff face to see her mansion, she would've recognized that beach; she'd ordered half a million dollars' worth of Hawaiian grass huts to serve limoncello under during the summer. They were still flapping there idly in the mist.

"Alright, keep them kneeling," she meant the mercenaries, kneeling, "till Derkans relieves you." Then she bounded back into the ship's interior to relay orders to Derkans as well. "Pilot this," she meant the ship, "to a hospital. Get them arrested." She meant the mercenaries. That way, at least, they might salvage some proof of French collusion.

But Derkans and Perkinze would need all the manpower they could get, stabilizing Spitz and Sfeder; one man couldn't exactly pilot a ship and guard mercenaries simultaneously. Visen'd have to go save Nadia and the secret documents on her own.

She told Derkans her plan, to let him know she was off, then dived from the ship's stern and started swimming.

If Nadia made it home, Visen had a good idea where she'd try to hide from the six shadowy gunmen who were even now making their way towards her mansion as well.

And Visen had had the bright idea to boast about Nadia's secret hiding place so the entire world— including Jacobsan and his goons, most likely— could hear.

Chapter 48

As Nadia swam, she had indeed been experiencing the weirdest de-ja-vu ever. At first, she thought maybe it was just the bright flare from the lighthouse, stunning her. Then she thought the shock from dodging bullets might've made the land seem slightly familiar; maybe a flight-or-fight response could trigger the misfiring of neurons that mistakes present for past.

As far as she could tell, when she'd first dived in the water, they were somewhere off the coast of Swiverlia; she'd planned to run to the nearest police station, or hitchhike, having fled precisely as she'd promised Visen she would, to let the professionals do their thing.

She was already regretting the three-inch long nails, that dragged ripplingly through the water as she paddled, but she was determined not to admit this to herself. It was her husband's fault for saying they made her look like a whore. If he hadn't been mean, she wouldn't have felt the need to counter with stubbornness to preserve her own sanity by protecting her own sense of self. So typical that Ivle's insults should egg her into doing something that slowed her down—

O-o-oh shit—what the? —And that was when she realized: they were in front of her own private beach head.

What the fuck? Where were they? That wasn't just a peninsula that looked like the one she swam past every summer; those were the grass huts she'd ordered last summer! How long had they been on that boat?

How far had she swum?

She turned to see the half-burnt cruiser about half a mile out from where she was now; it must have floated along with her towards the shore; it certainly wasn't being steered by any conscious entity. She reckoned she'd got in a good two miles' swim.

But those were definitely her tiki-huts. The weirdness drew her up short for a second, doggy paddling a sweeped, squidish movement backward in the water.

Alright. Alright fine. Easier to get help that way; she'd just have to find Wheeler. She kept swimming.

The water did actually feel wonderful —aside from how it tugged at her nails. Honestly, it was absolutely liberating not to have any clothes on, nothing to distract from the rippling liquid caressing her curves—probably kept her sane, by giving her the shock of a new sensation to recalibrate her senses while they shot at her— even if, now she'd reached the shoreline, clambering over pebbles without any shoes on really was hurting her feet—

Dammit! She'd told Ivle they needed to import sand…. She snuck into the pine trees dotting a sharp incline toward their backyard, aiming for the boathouse—now empty, since it was off season—that loomed large enough to fit A frame cranes for hoisting yachts in and out of the water, far off to the right-hand side of their property.

It was too foggy to see even half a mile down the beach, but some prehensile instinct hurried her along anyway, hunching itself in preparation for more gunshots.

She really wasn't wondering why people were trying to shoot at her. She didn't have time to. She just knew that they were.

She slipped in behind the boat house's blue wooden slating, hips on par with the greenish mold just faintly making inroads against the garden crew's hard-won cleaning. The empty docking space lapped idly round mossy rocks below its planking, deflected waves churning brown algae through the water.

She could hear feet stomping through the evergreens outside.

"Where the fuck did she go?"

"I thought you said there was a stairway,"

"Let's just go straight up," it was a bit of a hike from the beachhead to anywhere civilized.

"It's too wet; we get in there all soggy we're fucked,"

"Blurs DNA,"
"No it doesn't; it makes a fucking mess,"
"Here alright you stay here; see if she went around back—"
"We'll go back; it's gotta be by the tiki huts,"
There was a staircase by the tiki huts.

But Nadia knew a faster way home through the woods. She found her old dock-shoes in a corner and put them on, the minute crashing twigs signaled her hunters'd split up, hoping the sound of their own movement would keep them from hearing hers— then she ran for it through the trees—for about two minutes and then she just took to walking very quickly trying to hide how loudly she was breathing, fully conscious she didn't blend in well with the foliage, no matter how much she tensed her neck. Damn, swimming was so much easier than aerobic exercise that involved hurtling your entire bodyweight uphill against gravity.

She got to a French window at the side of the house. It was locked. Oh god dammit! She went round back to get a spare key. Round back felt so far. She was starting to get blisters from not wearing any socks.

Under the pot, next to the pansies—she didn't know why her hands had to be so fumbly at the thought she was racing to outrun 6 murderous home-intruders.

Into the house she went, upstairs to her room—she heard a tinkle in the main foyer—someone had broken the windowpane beside the front door. They were in. No time for clothes! She rushed into the bathroom and slipped into her hiding place.

Chapter 49

Visen, meanwhile, made landfall. She didn't know about the stairs by the tiki-huts or the short cut through the back woods; she just scaled the nearest cliff, hoping the gun she'd commandeered from her would-be captors was un-Mertrian enough to still work after having swum with it through sea water.

Ok. She paused for breath. Fog clung to her clothes. She surveyed the land, then sprinted across the lawns to the mansion's open front door. The window beside it had been smashed, glass twinkled where it fell across the main foyer.

Apparently Ivle hadn't given much thought to what would happen should his attackers come by sea. The formidable guard-gate ran all the way down, in both directions, to the water's edge and then stopped some thirty feet out. Of course, a row of thermal-sensors under water had been picking up all the scurrying activity round the beach-head for the last thirty minutes; Wheeler'd called the local constabulary, been told the break in had already been reported, rounded up the other three guards on site that day, and promptly been incapacitated by a fist to the face when he rounded the nearest corner after leaving the 'bullpen.'

All three guards were now being held face down in the gravel outside Nadia's mansion at gun point by one of the six shadowy home invaders.

But their guard hadn't expected anyone to pop up from the cliff to his right and make a beeline for the front door. Honestly, he was so busy scanning the tree lined driveway for the first signs of a patrol car's siren, he didn't notice Visen's grass-hushed rush to slip sideways through the entryway. And Visen was too busy calculating what to do next to take in Wheeler's predicament any more than registering his hostage situation as three assets she could free to use later.

She needed to secure Nadia and the paperwork Smutt hoped to steal first—wherever both might be. Nadia first: she wouldn't have had time to reach the guards' on-sight housing, not if thugs had already incapacitated Wheeler's team; she would have seen mercenaries controlled that sector of the grounds, and she would've known she'd have to pass through their cordon to make a run for it across country. Up against a hit-team of professional athletes, Nadia deciding on that course of action seemed unlikely. That would leave only the hidey-hole for safety, which meant Visen first and foremost needed to make sure no intruders made their way to Nadia's bathroom, in case they had learned where Nadia was most likely to secret herself away, either from Ivle's complaints to Jacobsan, which, now Visen thought about it, undoubtedly entered documentation for divorce proceedings the instant she'd proven his wife was spying on him, or—somehow worse—from Visen's double betrayal of Nadia's hidey-hole's location by talking about its location in a room full of people!

From Nadia's bathroom she could then smash through to Ivle's study and ask Nadia to find whatever paperwork proved Ivle's nefariousness. She'd keep it safe for Corvan to find; she wanted Corvan to get that paperwork, not some man who claimed to be working for France while breaking every UN peacekeeping protocol Visen had ever heard of.

To Nadia's bathroom then!

There was a surveillance panel in the solarium that should set her out right in front of the door to Nadia's room upstairs. She took the chance. She hopped up on a deck chair. She blasted her way through the second story's floor, lifting her body up through the hole in its wooden paneling.

Nadia's door was open; Visen could see through to the bathroom where one of the mercenaries was just now prying open the back panel to Nadia's lowest towel shelf.

"Alright little bitch time to—"

"Oi!" Visen shot him in the leg and tugged him out by the belt. The belt failed. Typical Mertrian! —Tons of little utility pockets and a buckle that didn't—actually maybe it was designed to do that on purpose. She dragged the rest of him out by the sheer force of digging her claws into reigning in the back of his combat suit.

He punched her in the chin; she punched him back; they rolled, bonking pipes. Eighteen aerosol hairsprays, perched claustrophobically atop the toilet Visen's head had bumped, joined in the fray. He elbowed her stomach; she grabbed his hair and whacked his forehead against the bathroom tiling, until he stopped moving.

"Nadia!" she crawled over him and wrenched open the back paneling to the towel shelf. Nadia wasn't there.

Chapter 50

"Nadia?" She pushed her hand through to the far backing of the rectangular abscess, dark enough, as it was, she may have overlooked— "Nadia?!"

"I'm in here!" came very muffled from the wood on all four sides of Visen.

"Where?" she ducked completely into the enclave, crouch pushing a shoulder against the far wall as she felt round its sides.

The cabinet under-running Ivle's third bookcase to the left idled open.

"That's it! That's gotta be it!" Four unaccounted for marauders had been rummaging through Ivle's study for signs of a secret compartment, pressing any button or knobbish-looking echelon they could find. They didn't know what they'd done to make the cabinet pop open, but they figured they'd finally pushed the right button.

Visen snuck back into the cabinet's shadows, and closed the towel shelf's paneling behind her, enveloping her silhouette in darkness.

One of the hitmen came over to look in the cabinet. Visen sat perfectly still, waiting, as he opened the drawer a crack further. She rammed the butt of her rifle into his face, rearing him back into a second investigator, who'd come to peer over his shoulder, stumbling the two of them back far enough she had space to crash through the cabinet's spindly facade and still site her gun's barrel directly into the nearest one's face.

A third turned and fired from where he stood by Ivle's desk; Visen dodged aside, books exploding into dust, right behind where her head had been —that meant they aimed to kill— just as the man she'd hit grabbed away her rifle. She used the off-balance tug as leverage; swung round his side and struck him with the back of her upper arm, crashing him down to the ground with a second jab to his temple, then falling atop him to lock his head between the rug and her armpit, grabbing the gun he held in the back of his belt to shoot back at the man who'd shot at her.

He ducked into an alcove, reappearing to take pot shots as the 2nd man at the cabinets hurled a chair over Visen's back; she broke the shock with an arch sideways to keep an arm between her head and the wood; letting it splinter round her, eyes squinched shut for only the moment of impact, then bursting round, off the man she'd floored, to grab the other's outstretched hand, where he was still holding, off balanced, three chair legs and the only two stretchers that spanned between them, which walloping Visen hadn't exploded apart.

She shot the man on the ground; she whipped the chair-wielder round to take a bullet in his back that'd been intended for her; she kept him raised and returned into her cabinet, blocking its entry with his body.

Inside Ivle's office, the one remaining assailant clicked three times at a button on his vest, to call in back up. They'd heard Ivle's place was hard to enter; they'd planned exactly what to do, should the first wave of intruders not suffice.

In fact, for the intruders, it was good timing. Out in the courtyard, Wheeler'd just gotten himself free, by waiting till the lone sentry set over him and his men had taken to pacing, trailing his semi-automatic from where he'd relaxed it into the crook of one elbow. Wheeler waited, timing how it took him about ten seconds each strut out to turn back, until the gun drew level with where he'd obediently smushed one eye into the gravel. The other eye swiveled, waiting for the man to come stand again, momentarily, by his head.

Then he pounced, grabbing at the gun's barrel, standing to Heimlich the sentry with one foot, when he bent after Wheeler's unexpected tug, instinctively refusing to relinquish his weapon.

He tried to push a button on his vest, but Wheeler's men were up in a second to subdue him. Ivle's security guards weren't just private sector bouncers. Well, Mazen was, but Mazen was also from Chicago and had had guns pulled on him before—which was handy because the first two men to respond to the call for help from Visen's assailant mistook the outdoor sentry's plight as the one they'd been called in to fix.

They shot and hit Wheeler. He fell. (He'd be okay; but recuperation therapy cost thousands). Mazen, as Wheeler's second, felt obligated to give up any sleight of hand he might have played to escape, and kneel by Wheeler's side to apply pressure; other hand in the air; "Don't shoot! Okay?" Now both hands in the air, one bloody. "Don't shoot!" Now one hand back down to apply pressure to Wheeler's wound.

The gunmen who'd fired turned out to be the first of 7 more assailants. They were getting in through a cave they'd carved out for themselves using dynamite. They had, after all, been planning to strike Ivle's house the morning after the gala for quite some time now.

The man out in front who'd shot Wheeler nodded towards the front door, for the six behind him to advance into the house. He and an eighth, whom Mazen hadn't seen before to count, raised rifles to their shoulders and stared down, hard and cold, at the little huddle of Ivle's security guards as Wheeler slowly bled out.

Ivle's study, of course, was so well sound-proofed no one inside heard the commotion. Visen's remaining antagonist crept carefully, silently, towards the cabinet through which she'd disappeared, wondering how long it took emergency backup to materialize.

He paused, then ducked his head and gun through the cabinet's splintered opening, all at once, savage and hate filled. No one there. Visen was standing next to the sink, with her rifle pointed at the hidey-hole's exit, waiting.

The mercenary lurched aside his dead companion, crawling through towards the sight of tiled bathroom just beyond; he'd been debriefed on the hiding place—Nadia was sure to be here somewhere.

Nadia's second hiding place, unfortunately, just on the other side of her sink, wasn't nearly as acoustically sealed as the library. She could hear every scraping scuffle of her searcher just a fiber board away, then a shot as he came through the wall and Visen permanently purloined any further search. He fell with a thud that shook her small hideaway's paneling.

"Ow! Jesus! So loud!"

"Where are you?"

"I'm in here; just next to you,"

"Where?"

"Under the sink; open up the sink cabinet,"

Visen open the small stand-alone cupboard that doubled as washstand to find, behind an s-trap in the plumbing, about 18 shampoos and facial cream bottles. The oak paneling at the cabinet's back was rising, ever so slightly.

"How many of these little spots do you have?"

"Seventeen."

"Okay—"

They could hear rushing footsteps downstairs. Visen whirled round. "Stay there!" She checked back to see the oak panel slink shut again quickly.

Now who was that coming now? Visen ducked back into the library and stole every gun she could find, along with every spare bullet. She had to double check how the second perp's pistol reloaded; it was an odd model—

Whoever was coming had found their way to the landing just outside. Visen could hear them panting. She hid.

Oh, that's why it was an odd model; it could be converted into a drill bit; why would anyone—? Stupid.

She snuck behind the outcropping of bookshelf nearest Nadia's new hide out and chose her third kill's rifle as primary weapon instead.

Five men burst in through the study's far door, just as two more burst through to Nadia's bedroom. Shit! This was not good.

They'd even picked up spare backup, by running into a guy from the first wave who'd been casing the kitchens.

"Cordova!" one of them called. Cordova, apparently, was the name of the guy Visen'd knocked out cold in the bathroom.

"Come on, come on man—" they slapped at him till he blinked into groaning.

"That bitch got my leg—"

Great! Visen knew she should've just killed him! Now they knew her approximate height and build. Fuck.

She kept listening.

"A'right hold still—"

"It hurts!"

"Jesus! Stop squirming—count to ten!"

"Ow! Ow ow ow ow ow!" They appeared to be applying either iodine or pressure.

The other man who'd entered Nadia's suite came back to rejoin the five in Ivle's study. But they weren't ransacking any more. This was a search and sweep; Visen could see by the way they flipped aside extraneous chairs when she peaked out for a second. They'd been forewarned that someone was in there waiting for them. It was only a matter of time before they realized Cicero's bust wasn't alone in its enclave.

The first man who realized got shot in the face. "Hey!" That brought the rest running over, leaving, apparently, the hapless Cordova to care for his own iodine.

Visen shot the second; she shot the third; the fourth shot straight at her heart but she caught it with her arm; the arm shattered, so she brought out a pistol to replace the rifle and shot back. They shot her in the leg; she whipped her pistol out of reach just in time as they grappled, ramming the bust of Cicero between her and a sixth, who shot off Cicero's nose, plaster scraping across Visen's face. She buckled down into leaning against the bookcase and kept firing. Five shots left; she'd checked the barrel: one to the face for an assassin she recognized; one to destroy the rifle another pointed at her, just as a third man grabbed her bloodied hair and jerked her head back to slash at her neck, but Visen was faster—she mirrored his movement to swipe the butt of her gun against the side of his neck; the sudden shock sent him stumbling.

Another tackled her; they were too close to shoot and know where the bullet would go, but she shot blindly anyway; a man who'd just reached out to grab her good arm fell; she used that arm's freedom to elbow away the man who had her pinned down, but this only ricocheted him up to shoot her twice in the lungs.

The sound of an ambulance wafted through the windowpanes. Cicero had smashed through Ivle's soundproofing.

"Get the papers!"

"Janx hadn't found 'em yet!"

"If that's the bodyguard the wife's still here! Search the house! No one leaves alive, understand?"

"Hah!" one of the mercenaries had been clawing desperately round the confines of Ivle's solid steel, old school art deco brutalism of a desk, and now his searching fingers finally hit against the button their prior search team had been hoping they'd found when Visen first attacked.

A compartment in the desk's sleek grey backing tipped out sideways, till it hit the obsidian wall, to reveal a mass of indexed blueprints, identical to those Colby was meant to order Crassburger to store amidst Mertria's governmental servers. The original floppy, used to monitor any subsequent sister files, was there too.

But Visen didn't see it. She could only hear the blood rattling in her lungs, and feel, with a vague sense of abandon, that once those documents were gone, there'd be no way to back up the Mertrian generals' statement to the press; Ivle could continue as interim president, and remain controlled by whoever was evil enough—UN or no—to decide wives counted as collateral damage.

"Thought she said it'd be in front?" the successful button-pusher had pressed a button hidden in the desk's back.

"'ll keep searching maybe there's more,"

"Check the cabinets and search the house!"

"Double check that that may be important—"

"And check upstairs; she might be in the—" their leader gestured to move them out without expending unnecessary energy talking, a sharp jerk of his hand paralleling where they knew from blueprints, they'd find a hallway upstairs.

Local constabulary had responded to an active shooter situation by surrounding the house with large megaphones and asking if they could talk to the perpetrators. Their intervention came wafting through the windows only as so much background noise. Negotiation wasn't what these men wanted. It just bought the ransackers more time.

"Alright come on; check the fucking compost; Sven saw her head here,"

One final intruder remained in the library, ransacking everything not already ransacked to make sure they hadn't missed anything. He started tearing books off the shelves at the room's far end. They weren't even actual books—they'd been cut in half, just used for aesthetics—wait. He seemed to have discovered where Ivle kept his portfolios documenting blackmailed subordinates. From where she lay, Visen could see pictures of service men paper clipped to reports. Come to think of it— Badmonkof's men had found that stash of folders too. Seriously? They hadn't considered blackmail incriminating?

The mercenary stacked the folders atop the secret paperwork from Ivle's desk panel, all of which had been splayed across his desk, to be added to as needed. Visen could see a trail of microfilm caught up uneasily over the secret compartment's edge, half squashed by reclosing the panel over its ribbon.

If only Visen could get those files. That had to be the mother file for the powerplant Nadia'd described; it was the only microfilm there. That'd be enough to jail Ivle. There were floppy disks in that pile too; she'd noticed the sound they made when they hit the table.

Obsolete on purpose, she'd bet anything— but technology that old would still contain enough identifying metadata to ensure prosecutors knew the documents originated from Ivle's computer. Visen knew for sure it would; floppies were the only type of data transfer system Mertrian SEALs' outdated protocols trained them to work with. Seemed for once Mertrians weren't the ones who could use a refresher on the specifics of computer capabilities.

Visen crawled with her one good elbow to take up defensive position as a sniper along the contours of Ivle's desk. Didn't matter that the shoulder she used to hold the rifle was shattered. She'd always experienced more pain than her fellow SEALs. She'd always had to carry more than a proportionate percentage of her body weight.

The trigger slammed the rifle's butt into her shoulder and a bullet through the final searcher's brain. She clawed the paperwork and floppies off the table with her one good hand; it was only a matter of seconds before searchers responded to the echoing report.

"Nadia," she drug and shoved and pushed her body and the paperwork over to the towel hideaway's hole; didn't matter if the pages tore; didn't matter if they wrinkled; didn't matter if they were out of order, they could ensure Nadia diplomatic immunity— Visen's brain wasn't even working well enough to register why this last was so important. She just knew it meant they could never hunt for Nadia like this again. "Take the papers—" she pushed them through the hole that now lay open into the bathroom and collapsed, head on par with the line that changed from roughshod wood to finished tile flooring.

Chapter 51

Boots appeared. Oh, fucking Cordova. She shot his foot. He fell. She shot his head. Now she was out of bullets.

"Visen!"

"Yeah?"

"Get back in here," a side panel opened up connecting Nadia's sink cupboard with the secret towel-shelf hideaway. Nadia's face, crouched over a thigh, was all Visen could see. "Come in the hide out with me!"

"Nadia."

Visen knew she would die. The only reason she hadn't died yet was because they'd punctured her lungs, not her heart. Lucky shot. Meant she got to die slower.

"Oh shit," Nadia hadn't realized Visen could lose.

She could see the gurgle of blood round her wound each time she breathed in.

"Take these; close the paneling. They're coming," Visen pushed the papers over almost one by one, till Nadia scuffed them all into her hiding place on the double, glancing nervously out at all the dead bodies speckled round.

No one came. They'd mistaken the shot for another scuffle on the driveway.

Nadia lowered the sink cupboard's side paneling at a whined "close the—outta—" Visen struggling to communicate displeasure, until only half an inch of an opening was left, to show where Nadia hid. "Watch for the coast to be clear. Then go out. Into the hallway." Visen knew Nadia could hear her through the woodwork, but her side-panel opened back up anyway, to peer an eye and nose out to be next to Visen's forehead, ostensibly to hear even better what she wanted.

When Visen breathed in, the hole in her side breathed in as well, making a small, sucky noise like a burst balloon. Whenever she breathed out, it whiffled. But she wasn't breathing in and out very hard by now. "Go through the panel I left open in the hallway that leads down into the solarium. There's a window behind the steam bath. Get behind the steam bath. Signal for help. If the coast is clear, climb out that window. Police are here."

"Are you gonna be okay?"

"Yes. Take papers." She pulled half-conscious at the fanning, bloodied blueprints and floppy disks, whatever half spilled out of Nadia's sink hide out.

"I will. I love you,"

Someone burst into Ivle's study.

"I love you too."

"Eh! We got a second bogey! We got another bogey loose! Eric's dead!" They could hear frantic radioing.

"Go when they convene. If you come across one, duck back into the room you just came from. Play them off one another."

Both were straining, now, to hear the coming footsteps, trying to count as they grew closer, and guess the positions of all those running, well-armed strongmen, hoping the jut of Visen's legs through the side paneling would be taken as just another casualty, to hide the fact a second person crouched beside her.

"Do you trust me?" Nadia barely mouthed.

"Hm?"

"Do you trust me?"

"Mm…."

Nadia opened the under-sink exit to her little hive and slunk round the shampoo to stand upright, then dived through her bedroom after her purse, scooping up as many hairspray cans as she could find along the way and coming back to deposit them beside Visen.

She fumbled out a credit card from the Gucci wallet she'd collected and shoved it hard against Visen's lung, straight into where the bubbling came through Visen's shirt. The whiffling stopped. Visen could breathe a bit better.

"See? I told you I was good at using credit cards, remember?" she'd read that survival tip in a magazine for boys once when she'd been thinking about having kids. She kissed Visen's cheek, tears almost coming out of her eyes, but she managed to make sure her grin remained stable.

"Why are you naked?" was the last confusion Visen could voice before her eyes bleared into half-closed oblivion, and all the focus of her life went into holding the credit card against her lungs, where Nadia had placed her bloody hands. In and out, in and out, until the gurgling in her lungs faded out of any register Nadia could hear, just as footsteps clunked into her bedroom, searching for whatever shooter had killed Eric on the sly.

"Cordova?" The man called out. Nadia could see him through the open door to her room, doubling back to check under the bed for Ivle's wife.

She grabbed Cordova's belt and fastened it round her waist, stuffing between it and her skin all the aerosol cans she could find. She had already grabbed her secret shame lighter for cigarettes she just couldn't resist out of its secret corner in her purse. Now she gripped it, and one last aerosol can she couldn't fit.

The man in the bedroom seemed to sense there was someone else, standing nearby. He straightened and crept closer. The bathroom door creaked as Nadia crept closer on its other side.

He paused, head tilted to hear better, ear towards the door. A low, roaring hiss of a sound at waist height reared to the flushing woosh of flames rushed together, as a skinny, tanned form sprang out of the bathroom.

Nadia held the aerosol's nozzle open till she felt the stream's pressure grow faint; still she held it; he couldn't bring his gun up to shoot as long as flames licked his face.

"Fuck!"

It wasn't just defense; it was revenge, for the breath that had faded out of Visen's chest. Nothing else seemed to matter.

Flames caught at his skin and his hair as she dropped the empty can and pulled out a new one—just in time. He'd lashed the flames out of his eyebrows with a frantic twist against the sleeve of his jacket—

He pulled a gun, but she tilted her new aerosol's flame down to bite into the flesh of his hand, then his neck—drive him back, till she conked him on the head with its empty cannister and pulled out a third one, to crouch over his motionless body, because more intruders were coming. She could hear them, on the far side of the wall.

Up she leapt, slamming the bathroom door shut as she passed into her bedroom. Out of sight, out of mind—if it worked for her laptop in the Superstore parking lot, it'd work for Visen. She crept to the side of her bedroom's entryway. The first responder entered, gun drawn—instantly flamed in the back by an aerosol can and her lighter. He pivoted, raking bullets over the wall, but Nadia pivoted with him, keeping up the can's steady flow till his skin lit and instinct dropped the gun to clutch at his flames. Now she had a gun. She'd gone skeet shooting before—but, no, bad idea. She dropped back, sneaking the gun alongside her naked tiptoe forward as collateral, until she sprang with a click of the door closed behind her into the closet where she'd hidden from Ivle all the paraffin she'd bought, by storing it behind her shoes.

Coughs at smoke in the hallway promised the remaining intruders were coming.

They'd stationed two down front to aid Wheeler's guard in keeping the police well back from aiding him, but they'd also snuck round to the east of the house and through a back door.

She needed to act fast, in case her second casualty's head burnt out.

"What happen—"

"The wife! Fucking wife!"

"Where is she?"

"In there! In there!"

Nadia didn't hear them any more than the far-off echoes of a Zen master's meditation; she knew they were closing, but she no longer cared to count the locations they were coming from. She grabbed the torch she'd been taught to make, soaked it in paraffin, shook it impatiently over her shoes, to free it of excess oil, lit it, sucked in a long drawn breath through her nose, poured paraffin into the gulpy frog-face she'd learned to make with her mouth, wiped her chin on her shoulder, ripped open the closet door, and blew like a dragon except the look on her face spelled out infinitely more voraciously "fuck you."

Fire swallowed up the first two men, forcing them back, while it licked round the closet door's mantel. Nadia didn't want to have her back exposed, but she didn't want fire to catch her in the closet, so she kept walking forward, torch brandished like a scimitar, fire three feet in front of her, sweeping low and sideways, in the measured exhale she'd learned from breathing bubbles for her face exercises.

As she pivoted, she unscrewed with one hand the next cannister of paraffin, pouring a line of alcohol along the rug as she stalked. Up it went in flames, a buffer between them and her. But someone had already gotten behind, and now grabbed her arm. She rounded and rammed the torch's burning wick against his forehead, flourished like a baton to shove him back in agony, but that only made way for the next, who didn't realize she still had fuel to breath out. Her skin-melting roared against him, straight in the face.

Oh my God, this was fun! Also, her hair was on fire. She stopped exhaling for only a second; a paraffin bottle replaced the lighter in her left hand as she chugged, waving the still lit torch before her to set on fire whatever else she could reach.

Three shots as she ducked down to one side, but she moved so continuously within the ripple of smoke they shot blindly, the fire in their eyes; the nearest's cowlick burst into flames.

For one weird moment it was difficult to tell where the fire ended and Nadia began; her hair had frizzled to one side (Perry's Make-Do-A-Day Hair Moisturizer had proven unnaturally flame retardant), as she leapt over licks of flame to spray more across her bedroom— now they were cut off from Visen.

But if the image of Nadia shocked, it only shocked for a second; one mercenary raised his rifle now to fire at close range; the torch crashed down against its barrel in a crazed push to one side, oil running its flaming wick straight into his shoulder, as Nadia drew closer than could allow a rifle's barrel between them. She whipped the torch round to hold like a javelin and jammed it against the hair on the back of his head, forcing him towards her, till he stood between nails and fire, to shield Nadia from the four shooters who'd heard calls for help and just rounded the corner.

Ok. Fuck that shit about spitting in a straight line. She dunked paraffin on the twisting man between her and her would-be attackers, and rubbed the torch's wick over him to make sure it lit, then tilted paraffin between her lips and blew it out like a pivoting sprinkler, fire lashing out for long enough it drenched the room in flames; she could run past it to stand behind another man still shooting at its dying plumes. The fire choked and babbled, and began to catch at vanity stands.

She burst from the room's atrium, back towards her four poster bed, scorching its polyester drapes as she ducked to let bullets pass over her, flailing the torch to catch their melting fall, so she could spin it at the nearest crouching gunner as a jabbing flail to knock him back, before he could aim his sites round her bed.

They were fully in her room now, silent, blackened silhouettes; she only hoped the bathroom door could hold against flames, keep Visen preserved. All round it now billowed in torrents, flames lisping back towards the windows that were her last means of escape this side of the smoke curtain.

They needed to stop the blaze— two searchers from Ivle's library came running, stuffing important looking documents down their shirts.

"Hey! What—? The—?"

It was like whack-a-mole, but with guns and a burning torch.

A third, cut off from the others, knocked Nadia down to the floor, but she doused him in a jug's flip of paraffin and pressed the torch against his skin, leaping up, the last of her misting vapor spraying heat against his head till he backed into the wall; his comrades could see him struggle, but they couldn't reach him; the wall of flame grew higher, till tears poured out of Nadia's eyes, contacts no longer any protection against engulfing smoke. But this wasn't survival; it was aristeia. She could stand there all day; the plaster behind the body she held was starting to burn.

Visen could hear shouts; she felt the heat of encroaching fire. Something fell outside the bathroom door. She crammed the floppy disks Nadia's sink hide out still held under her body as dark plumes of smoke began billowing out of the mansion's east end. "Fire! Get the Fire Department!" Radios began crackling commands.

By now, Nadia was lighting everything she could on fire. She was most vulnerable while refueling; that was when they could shoot her, the ring of eight men who'd come running to execute and been blinded instead, rustled into grasping one another and pulling injured comrades out of the flames.

In the confusion, one of the men who had appeared now shot the man nearest Nadia. She paused, but the gun raised again; the bullet had been meant for her, a wave of piercing smoke had simply tugged at his lungs till he mis-calibrated.

Another blanket of flame and she hopped out the window, just a floor above where Visen had told her to go. Out onto the unnecessarily balustraded ledge that ran the length of their upper stories. Now she could keep up a wall of flame against them until the paraffin ran out. But Visen was still inside—

"Help!" she wasted a teaspoon of paraffin, spitting it out to call: "Help!" the firefighters had just pulled up, but been warned, as it was a hostage situation, they could at best only operate from three meters away, or risk instant casualties in the form of flying bullets.

They saw her. The police saw her too. The men inside could tell where she stood based on which direction the fire flared from, but the angle needed to hold a gun out the window was awkward enough Nadia could rip away any they pointed at her. She did so. Ok, she'd seen movies. She stuck the semi-automatic they'd just forfeited back in through the window and pulled the trigger, firing at random. The recoil almost knocked her off the ledge. She got a better hold, then spewed bullets again, back and forth, till she could duck down and get a good look at the room, just as one assailant ducked back behind her dresser; she shot him before her brain could analyze what movement she'd seen. No others? There were four men lying blasted through by the window.

A fifth was ramming his way through the bathroom door from a crouched side-crawl; he'd realized where the missing microfilm might've gone. No! She shot at him but the angle was off; she chugged more paraffin, exhaled a flame to cover her back, and turned round one last time to yell down at the driveway: "Oi! Help!" before descending down through the open window. Flame was just beginning to catch round its maw.

"They're all dead you stupid cowards!" she called back again through the window. Well, almost. Now to reach the man clunking through to her bathroom. She could see him; just barely warbled by flame; he'd punched in the bathroom door's central paneling—she shot.

"They're all dead!"

One wasn't. He didn't have a gun but he hadn't been stupid. As soon as Nadia wrenched the semi-automatic from his grasp he'd assumed returning fire would follow and dropped under her bed, instead of trying to grab his gun back through the open window like the rest of them.

Now he lunged to strangle her, but she twisted round, bit him in the face and held on, teeth wrenched into his cheek—that got him to let go—as he tried to pummel her away with fists and elbows now. She kneed him in the groin and grabbed at his eyes with tensed fingers, but he caught one of her arms and managed to tear away; she'd ripped a chunk of flesh off his face. She spat it back at his nose, then started kicking and seesawing, first her head butting forward, then her knee jabbing up, then her head butting forward, like some warped calisthenics, all while on fire and flailing nails.

By then the firemen had reached the balustrade. They didn't see any guns, they just saw a man attacking a naked woman and leapt in to drag him off, threatening him with the ax they'd brought.

"Maim! Are you alright? You alright?"

She grinned up at them a shapeless show of bloody, smeared teeth. "Don't worry; it's not my blood,"

"Ew."

The black specks had begun to part from Nadia's vision, as her drapes soaked down from flames to puddles—the firemen'd brought a hose with them as well— she finally caught a gasp of fresh air.

"My girlfriend's in the bathroom!"

Flames still leapt and crackled from that quadrant of the room. Fire boots and snaking hose darted to rescue Visen. "She's been shot through the lungs!"

She was still holding Nadia's credit card to her wound. The whole thing had taken about five minutes.

"No don't!" Visen could see the hose tipping towards her and ripped upward in one hand what she could of the blueprints and floppy disks. "These need to be saved; they're evidence; you have to save—!" she passed out, just as Nadia ran in through the massed firemen to round up Visen's precious paperwork and keep it safe. "Got it! Get her!" she ran back out again, legs scampering under a clutched maelstrom of seeming office supplies. The nuclear blueprints may have been caked in blood and ripped, but they would be enough to go on—once Visen got Max to repair the incriminating floppy disks that went along with them.

Chapter 52

Nadia sat by Visen impatiently, the whole five days she was comatose, like she had a wonderful joke to tell someone, but only Visen could appreciate it.

"So!"

As soon as she opened her eyes, Visen saw the burned, bruised, manic face of Ivle's wife.

"Nadia?"

"Guess what was actually really fun and invigorating? I think, for our next date, we should go to a nudist colony!"

"What happened?"

"Oh my god! So!" And, like Beowulf's immortal bard, Nadia was off to fill in all the details.

~*~

She and Evelle were divorced by the following month.

One of Nadia's friends ended up buying their house. Which really helped Ivle with all his legal fees, considering every single lawyer he knew who specialized in Mertrian law ended up going to jail as well, headed, as they were, by Jacobsan.

At first, standing as a witness to help convict Ivle proved tedious, and Nadia grew to dread the thought she'd be in court even on days when her divorce wasn't being processed. Then, she realized she could embellish everything, so long as the details were truthful, and get an entire courtroom to listen to her as though she were Cat-woman. After that things went off with a blast. She even wanted to testify in appeals court, but apparently that wasn't required.

Max eventually turned tail and reported his position in the scheme of things. Turned out he'd been blackmailed for drugs too; Speed.

In the end, an entire pyramid scheme of rotten lawyers and blackmailers went to jail, except for one of Ivle's consulting property lawyers named Polips, who got off by striking a deal with the state.

Turned out, he'd been the one responsible for ensuring local police didn't detain the burglar Wheeler'd caught. It hadn't only been bribery and corruption that got the guy free, there'd also been some wickedly good legal parlance too, apparently— legal parlance Polips now turned to his own advantage.

Ivle hadn't known one of his subordinates actively aided those caught breaking and entering in an attempt to abduct his wife, and he tried to pin evidence on Polips in revenge, which drastically backfired, and got him put away for extra time.

Visen, meanwhile, was put in the same rehabilitation classes as Wheeler. She had extra, additional breathing exercises for the punctured lung, but it turned out she'd been shot in almost precisely the same place on her leg as he had, which meant they could spend afternoons complaining about it together—at least one reasonably enjoyable outcome.

Nadia didn't get anywhere near the amount of alimony she'd been hoping for, when the divorce finally did come through (something about 'purposefully spying on one's spouse'—which seemed a bit hypocritical considering all the security cameras). But the friend who'd bought Ivle's mansion bought Nadia a small cottage on its grounds to move into— "see?" she'd told Visen, "I told you I have lots of friends I don't need to be a gold digger,"— which turned out to be much more manageable to decorate because by then Nadia was going through a minimalist phase.

Plus, she still had access to the solarium. And she bribed the cook to continue supplying her with food, which, it turned out, was actually just a perfectly legal business transaction, because the cook used part of the money to buy the ingredients she needed, and the only slightly-not-above-board complication came in the form of the cook using her new boss' kitchen for someone else's cooking, though, when Visen demanded this be disclosed, it turned out Nadia's friend didn't mind if they used the kitchen; she mainly survived on fruit anyway.

"We met in the same dietary restrictions class," Nadia explained.

"Mm."

Visen never could regain feeling in three fingers on her left hand, but Mertria offered her another medal, and 250$ for her trouble, which was somehow absolutely to be expected.

Nadia paid for the hospital bills.

"Now you can have sex with me and don't need to feel like you need to reciprocate while you heal! Because I paid, for this! For—you know, so we can have sex, because I wanted to."

"So, it's like you're—paying me to have sex with you?"

"No, it's like you're paying me to have sex with you!"

"What?"

"In a—metaphorical way. Also, I can give massages," Nadia squeezed the air in front of her.

They spent Visen's recuperation hiring consultants to create a costume for Nadia to perform fire-breathing in full time, but this somehow merged, halfway through, into a career as dominatrix instead, for which Nadia's friend allowed her use of the mansion's east wing as part of a 'fully immersive experience'.

After about five days ferrying paraffin for Nadia's more extravagant escapades—which turned out to be enormously popular—bumping along in an old truck from the paraffin emporium to Ivle's estate, though Nadia's providers were perfectly willing to truck the stuff over themselves for an extra 25$—Visen hobbled off and put in a transfer request to work from home for the SEALS, as a bit of a return to her old desk job. But, of course, now that the amphetamine usage was out, the military didn't really feel comfortable continuing any further relations with her. They traded her an honorable discharge, instead, for not kicking up a stink about how the hospital's x-rays discovered deterioration in her knees directly correlatable to habitual over-usage in the SEALs.

Luckily, that career dead-ended only two hours before three consultants arrived from England to discuss whether Visen would like to purchase Ivle's thermal dynamics corporation for a nominal fee of 3 million dollars, which Nadia's friend instantly loaned, as it seemed like a very good deal. (Nadia's friend was named Slevanka and had enormously powerful connections in Russia).

So, Visen went into thermal defensive industries—about which, the consultants promised, Ivle had known absolutely nothing when he first began as well.

Ivle had, apparently, come to see that particular thermal defenses corporation as his own special baby, and he didn't want the company going to anyone who wouldn't be smart enough to know how to run it—hence his English lawyers arriving en masse at Visen's door; she was, after all, his most valuable asset.

So Visen, besieged by dubious business partners and uncertain primary motivations, found herself invited on hunting trips with good old boys who wanted to maintain connections with such a promising new field as thermal dynamics.

But that, and whether or not she ever got used to Nadia sneakily suggesting they try BDSM in the bedroom, is another story to tell altogether.